THE SEA of HOPE

by
JULIE SUWITRA

A catalogue record for this book is available from the National Library of Australia

Publisher:
Inspiring Publishers
P.O. Box 159, Calwell, ACT Australia 2905
Email: publishaspg@gmail.com
http://www.inspiringpublishers.com

National Library of Australia Cataloguing-in-Publication entry

Author: Suwitra, Julie

Title: **The Sea of Hope**/*Julie Suwitra*

ISBN: 978-1-922618-24-5 (pbk)

For my children, with love. Katherine, Justine, Putu Ariata dec. and Lily P

Author's Note

The hazardous, and desperate journeys taken by refugees across the Mediterranean Sea are real and ongoing. It should be the right of everyone to seek a safe and better life, sadly this is not always the case. Although the refugee situation is very real, this book is primarily a work of fiction, set in some real places.

About the Author

Julie Suwitra was born in Kyabram, a town in north central Victoria, Australia. For the past fifteen years she has lived on the island of Bali, Indonesia teaching English and History at a private school. She is a regular visitor to Italy, in particular Sicily where her novel is set. Since her retirement she spends her time between Australia, Bali and Italy. She is married and has three children and four grandchildren.

Acknowledgements

Thank you to my dear friend Hetty Hanstein for looking at a shambolic first draft and giving me hope. To my husband Ketut, for your patience and the endless plates of Nasi Goreng. To my daughter Lily P, for the beautiful book cover. To renowned Italian actor Cesare Bocci, thank you for your kindness on a hot dusty street in Scicli, Sicily, June 2019. To Il Maestro, Andrea Camilleri, I remain forever grateful for your inspiration. Last, but certainly not least, to the kind, generous people I have been fortunate to meet on my travels in Sicily. Grazii.

Chapter 1

Luminous starlight revealed a pathway that wound through the inky blackness down to the sea. Tough, stunted bushes lined the rugged shoreline ahead. Sheshy sighed, a mixture of exhaustion and gratitude. He had almost made it. 'Thank you, God,' he whispered as he followed the ragged group of people silently moving along the narrow path which led to the water's edge. Everyone was focused on reaching the beach and there was quiet determination to see this long journey through to the end. Occasionally a mother could be heard hushing her crying baby. Sometimes a hacking cough broke through the silence, a sound which came from a body already worn down by exhaustion, only the dream of a better life willing it on.

It had taken a long time to reach this place. Sheshy had finally left his small, continuously ransacked village in Eritrea six months ago. At first, he thought he could stay there and try to make a life for himself, but in the end, there was no choice but to leave. After Sheshy's parents died, his father murdered in a neighbourhood dispute, and his mother following close behind after having succumbed to complications bought on by the miscarriage of what would have been her eighth child, Sheshy knew he had to leave, even though it would be a long dangerous journey. What else was left for him in a country constantly at war? The endless search for non-existent work and scant food had left him desperate. All he wanted was the chance to live a decent life, so, he had sold what meagre belongings remained in the family's hut and left. His older brothers and sisters had gone long ago. He had no idea what had become of them. Their faces had gradually faded from his memory and now he no longer felt any attachment to them. The younger ones had been taken in by relatives, but at eighteen that wasn't an option for him. He was on his own.

After he left the village, he joined a group of people who were making their way through several countries that would eventually lead them to the Libyan coast. Hopefully, when they got there they would have enough money to pay a people smuggler to take them across the Mediterranean Sea to Europe. Up to this point, their journey had been long and arduous, through The Sudan and into Libya. Along the way some of the members of their group had perished, ten of them struck down by a mixed bag of illnesses. Exacerbated by years of poor nutrition, their immune systems were already compromised, so they had died from influenza, food poisoning or other ailments which in different circumstances they might have had a chance of surviving. For them, this journey had been the final straw, their bodies unable to keep up with the demands placed on them. Two women had died in childbirth and three elderly people from exhaustion. From a group that had started with fifty-five people, only forty remained when they finally reached the small town near the Libyan coast.

For several days they had waited in a dirty, crowded camp watched closely by other groups. It was common knowledge that there were people who waited in these camps, looking for an opportunity to take whatever possessions the migrants still had. Like vultures, they watched, on the lookout for any signs of vulnerability. Sheshy's group, which had formed a tenuous bond during the journey, took turns keeping watch. Guarding their possessions and protecting those who were more at risk from the predators who lurked at the edge of the campsite. They were constantly on the alert for any subtle changes in the camp's atmosphere. These could be new arrivals who didn't seem to be connected to any group and whose clothing was of better quality than what was normally worn by migrants and who wore expensive watches or jewellery. Gangs of stand over men and opportunists also waited, ready to take advantage of any change in the migrants' circumstances. They were often people who had been on this migration journey for years. People with nothing to lose. The past experiences of horrendous events and extreme hardship had driven them to a place where any previous feelings of moral responsibility had gone. It was every man, woman and child for themselves. Each day brought new challenges. Time was spent talking to people who could guide them to the boats and operators who managed them, then trying to negotiate the price. There was also the added stress of working out whether it was a genuine offer or just an opportunity to part them from their precious money.

The women had a far harder time, some of them dressed their daughters' in boys' clothing in an attempt to protect them from the leering looks and assaults which were commonplace and just a glance away. The predatory, direct stares which signalled the overt intentions of the men close by. Although they looked out for each other and fragile relationships were formed, it didn't pay to get too close, it wasn't worth the pain of another loss. It was best to look forward, forget about the past and focus on the life ahead. This was the only way to survive Sheshy thought.

Finally, word came, there was a boat leaving the next night, cash upfront, and no arguing.

Now here they were, this was it..... the end of one journey and the beginning of the next. Sheshy continued to follow the path down to the waiting boat.

When the group reached the men waiting on the shore, they caught their first glimpse of the vessel that was going to take them onwards to their final destination, and hopefully a better life. It looked flimsy and not particularly seaworthy, it certainly didn't inspire much confidence, but there was no alternative. The people gathered around the men who would take their money and give them a seat on the vessel. They were most likely fishermen who had found a more lucrative way to make money, not necessarily bad men, but just seizing an opportunity that had come, servicing a market...the helpless, desperate tide of humanity sweeping across Africa towards the utopia that was Europe. The journey was meant to take three to five days but who knew what could happen along the way. Sheshy knew that the sea in front of them was filled with the corpses of those who had died trying to get to safety, but there was no other choice. The boat didn't look capable of sailing with twenty people on board let alone forty, he hoped he would be one of the lucky ones and manage to get on board and find a safe place to sit. There didn't seem to be any life jackets either which made it all the more perilous.

'Aren't there any life jackets?' A voice spoke up from the back of the group.

'What do you expect for the amount you're paying us?' One of the men answered.

A couple of them looked unpleasant, thugs, there to make sure that if there were any protests they would be dealt with swiftly. Possibly Libyan, definitely people you wouldn't argue with.

They were quite dark with sinewy bodies and hard faces. The bulky shapes visible under their shirts were most likely weapons, knives, and possibly guns. The leader of the group had a soft-looking, fleshy mouth, occasionally a flash of gold glittered as his lip curled in what was meant to pass as a smile. It was always directed at one of the younger, prettier women. Sheshy felt sick with apprehension but forced his way to the front, his money well hidden in a cloth purse stowed under his new jacket, close to his skin. He had bought the jacket at the beginning of the journey using some of his precious money. Although it had cost more than he had wanted to spend, Sheshy knew it was a good investment. He was sure to get cold along the way, especially on the sea voyage and there was no doubt that a jacket would be necessary in the future.

'We agreed the price was four thousand dollars, is that right?' Sheshy ventured...

'I suppose so, where is it, have you got it?' One of the men asked, a greedy glint in his eye.

Sheshy pulled out the purse stuffed with notes and handed it to a man who appeared to be in charge of things. He grabbed it and shuffled the notes roughly. 'Ok get in the boat,' he barked.

Sheshy quickly made his way to the flimsy vessel, before the man in charge changed his mind or demanded more money. There he sat, his knees up under his chin trying to take up as little room as possible. Thankfully, he had managed to secure a place at the side, near the front, that way if he felt ill, or something happened on the voyage he might have a chance of saving himself. More people came on board. Suddenly harsh voices penetrated the night, one of the travellers was protesting that he had been promised, by a middle man, his children would only pay half price for the passage.

'It's all I have, please show mercy, please take us,' his cries rang out in desperation, tears falling down his hollow, lined cheeks. The months of travelling, the stress, and the fear which had followed them across the land finally reached its climax on the shore. Then there was the sound of a thud, something striking flesh, which made Sheshy turn and look back towards the rocky beach. Through the rapidly darkening dusk, he saw one of the men suddenly bring the thick side of an oar down on the side of the protesting man's head. He fell to the ground, the blows still raining down on him. His wife and two small children looking in horror as their husband and father's body lay feebly twitching on the sand in front of them. Too frightened to speak, they rocked backwards and forwards in mute grief and fear. Eventually, two men picked up the limp, lifeless body and threw it into the bushes behind them.

'Anyone else got anything to say?' The leader faced the group. His combative stance and hardened features leaving no doubt as to what any further dispute might lead to.

'Get rid of them,' he ordered, and the woman and children were dragged away into the darkness. He had already pocketed their money and now turned back to the others waiting to take their place on the boat. The rest of the payments were handed over in silence, and eventually, everyone was seated. No one spoke, their faces immobile and their slumped bodies too worn out to care anymore. It was everyone for themselves, driven by the will to survive. A few voices shouted out and the three men who would operate the boat jumped in and began to row out to deeper water. When they were far from the shore one of the men turned on the elderly, spluttering motor. I hope it makes it, Sheshy thought with some trepidation. At least the weather was ok, the middle of July was usually free of big storms and major weather events. He hoped so. He was one of the few people on board who could swim a bit, even so, he didn't like his chances of surviving an accident at sea. Let's hope the boat doesn't spring a leak or be tossed too roughly by a huge wave, he thought. The boat made it's way slowly through the night's blackness. The stars were brilliant above them and the brisk air made those who weren't properly dressed for the voyage, shiver, and hug their pitiful belongings closer to them. The lights from the shore slowly faded from sight and the boat gently tossed in the darkness surrounding them. People began to pray, words of hope and gentle pleas to their God to keep them safe. The sounds continued softly, drifting up into the night sky.

Sheshy must have dozed off, finally succumbing to the rhythmic rocking of the boat. The gentle murmur of people talking, combined with his own overwhelming mental and physical exhaustion had brought him the sleep he needed. When he awoke, the red rim of a fiery sun was coming up over the horizon, dawn was breaking and the start of a new day. He didn't know how long he had slept for, but it seemed like only a short time. His legs felt cramped and he longed to stand up and stretch them but he knew that was impossible, so he tried to massage them instead. The people around him were now silent, afraid to move incase the unseaworthy vessel suddenly keeled over and tossed them all down into the murky depths of the sea. Sheshy reached into his bag and took out a piece of bread, some hard cheese, and a bottle of water. He would have to restrict his food intake, as the meagre provisions he had brought with him had to last the days at sea. Others were waking around him, attempting to stretch in their confined space. He could see that a few of them were also suffering from cramps, especially the older people. Some of the younger ones attempted to massage the tired and arthritic limbs of their elders.

The endless, green expanse of the sea stretched out around them as far as the eye could see. There was no land in sight.

The old boat steered onwards, to what, no one knew, they just hoped it would be somewhere safe and welcoming.

'Ah! What do you think our chances are of making it to safety?' A prematurely aged man travelling with his small son, asked. 'I hope we make it. I have a cousin in Catania, in Sicily, who has promised me a job. There is just me and my son, the rest of my family including my wife and sister died on the journey from The Sudan.' He couldn't have been more than thirty-five, Sheshy thought, but he looked at least sixty-five. It was certainly true that a life of hardship made people age more quickly, unlike those who were lucky enough to live in more affluent countries.

'I pray that we will, but in the end, it is in God's hands isn't it?'

The man nodded silently and hugged his son to him.

The afternoon dragged on. The sun beat down, making those on board lethargic and nauseous. The precious water supply was to be drunk only when it was necessary. Several people, who were able to, hung their heads over the side of the boat, trying to catch the moist air rising from the waves lapping against it.

Towards nightfall, as the people were once again eating their slowly dwindling food, they began to notice that the wind was picking up. No longer a sea breeze it was rapidly becoming a strong and potentially dangerous threat to the people on that flimsy boat. Soon it started rocking erratically on the rising water, the increasing swells lifting the boat then bringing it down with a sudden, heaving thud. The waves crashed into the boat, making everyone sodden and overcome with fear. The violently tossed boat filled with the sound of peoples' cries, pleading with God to save them. Some passengers tried to move to the sides then vomited into the rolling waves, while others' cries grew louder. Suddenly the howling turned to screams. A wailing filled the air. Sheshi looked to the back of the boat and saw that a child had been picked up by a wave and tossed into the sea, it's distraught, grief-stricken mother was trying to follow the child into the churning, green sea. The people close to her were attempting to hold her back while they watched helplessly as the child disappeared below the white caps of the waves. Eventually, she was restrained and fell into a sobbing heap, comforted by members of her family.

To try and rescue the child would have been nothing short of a suicide mission. Anyone who could swim knew it was stupid to try, no matter how much they wanted to help. The horrific scene witnessed by those close by was mirrored on each person's face. They clung on to the sides of the boat, to each other, and to their faith, until finally at some point during the night the gods showed mercy. The strong winds abated and the rough sea gradually became calmer. The boat, at last, stopped it's relentless pitching and rolling. People sat exhausted, some with their heads pressed down on their knees, others with their bodies flung back, their energy depleted. They stayed like that throughout the rest of the night. There was little conversation, people taking comfort that the worst seemed to be over and they were still alive.

Finally, daylight crept over the horizon and they saw the outline of land in the distance. 'That must be Malta,' someone said, and gradually the expressions of fear and exhaustion lifted from many of the faces and were replaced with hope. The woman whose child had been swept overboard the night before was lying prone with grief at the feet of her husband, her body occasionally shuddered under the cloth which covered her.

Sheshy looked over towards Malta, not far now, he thought as he gazed at the misty tracing of land beyond the sea. The rest of the day passed without any more drama. As people began to feel more hopeful and the faint outline of Sicily appeared, the travellers started speaking more. Conversations between people forced into such intimate proximity were gentle and full of respect. Throughout the journey, everyone had tried not to cause a fuss, trying to get along and be there for each other. Sheshy had heard terrible stories told by others, of family and friends who had taken the same perilous journey. People had been so desperate they had pushed people out of the boat to make sure there was enough room for their family. Others had been robbed of what little they had, while they slept. Thankfully everyone was trying to be kind and show consideration towards each other, so far. Maybe the dreadful night in the pitching boat had made everyone grateful to have survived.

Night fell again and people were quiet. They could now make out distant lights and their hearts once again filled with hope. It would probably be only a few more hours before they landed, unless a police boat spotted them. Then they might either be hauled aboard the police boat, if it happened far out to sea, or if it was closer to shore, their boat would be attached to the police vessel and towed into the harbour with them on board. They would then be taken to an onshore processing centre. Who knows what would happen after that. Sheshy had heard stories of people taken to farms in parts of Sicily and made to work as indentured farmhands, little more than slaves. He had also heard of people who had been worked to death. Housed in subhuman conditions, given the bare minimum to eat, and watched constantly in case they tried to escape.

He didn't want that sort of life, he wanted to take a chance, to try and find his own way and be free no matter how hard it might turn out to be.

The lights drew closer, their twinkling reflected in the water. The effect was one of an almost partylike atmosphere. In another hour they would reach land.

In less than no time, the shore came up to meet them. One minute they were in deep water, the next they could feel rocks scraping the bottom of the boat. It pitched suddenly in the waves, making people grab the sides of the boat in desperation. It was very dark and even though there was a myriad of stars above them and a bright moon, it was still difficult to see. He could now make out what appeared to be some shadowy figures coming down to meet them.

Sheshy could hear loud voices. They seemed to be arguing violently about something. It sounded a bit like Italian but not quite. maybe Sicilian or a dialect from somewhere else. The people on board stayed where they were, not knowing what to do. Should they make a run for it or just sit and wait for the people arguing to work it out. Suddenly some of the men broke away from the others and started shooting into the boat. The bullets tore into the vessel and through the people sitting in it. A torrent of bullets fired from automatic weapons smashed through bodies leaving behind a destruction that was almost beyond belief, until you looked closely at the flesh which had been torn apart. Cries of disbelief turned to screams as loved ones were cut down in a hail of bullets. Sheshy could not understand. Why was this happening? He watched in horror, as the senseless carnage continued around him. Parents died trying to shield their children. Others attempted to escape, their bodies caught in mid-flight. Sheshy had no sooner looked around him when an incredible pain seared through his chest and then all went black.

He lay half inside the boat, the other half hanging over the side, his arm gently moving in the water. The new jacket was riddled with bullets, the water tuning red with blood in the surrounding sea.

Inside and around the destroyed boat, bloodied corpses lay, thrown haphazardly by the violence of the massacre. Men spoke in a harsh violent language. The seamen who had brought the boat to this destination were now lying on the rocky beach, their bodies thrown against rocks like discarded clothing. Some of the men went to the boat and tipped it over, corpses and possessions floated away, flotsam and jetsam tossed into the waves along with the other detritus that had come from the shore. A sad, sorry sight, such a waste of human life. All those hopes and dreams wiped out in a single moment. The men who had been responsible for this despicable act turned and walked back up the rocky path, the moonlight casting a yellow glow on the scene below and lighting their path ahead. All was quiet again.

Chapter 2

A strong morning light filtered through the soft, white curtains, it was going to be another hot day.

Susan had woken with a heavy head and heart. A feeling of inexplicable restlessness added to her despondent mood. She was a woman in a state of mental turmoil, a woman who, in two days, would turn seventy...seventy! Where on earth had the time gone? One minute she was young, giving little thought to what lay ahead, caught up in the day to day running of her life. A busy mother of three grown up children, an amicable divorce behind her, working in a job that she loved and engaged in a full life. Now she was turning seventy, a number which held a certain fear, a feeling that when the clock finally ticked over something dreadful would happen. She tried to calm herself by thinking about all the bright, creative women over seventy. Fashion designers, actresses, scientists, politicians...... They were all still making a difference, contributing to the world. They didn't suddenly stop working, stop creating, why couldn't she feel the same. She wasn't ill, she was still alive, plenty of her friends hadn't made it this far. It was just a bit too much to handle. I think it's the number, just saying it made her feel old and redundant. No matter how many times you heard, 'Oh, seventy is the new fifty,' it was still seventy, even if you felt like fifty. Susan tried to exercise everyday, ate a mainly vegetarian diet and didn't drink too much alcohol. She tried to practice mindfulness and took furtive looks at her horoscope, when she remembered. In the end it was probably best to not dwell on it too much. She would try to spend the day doing something she loved. After all, she was in the best place.

Susan had first travelled to Italy only a few years ago. She had spent a lot of time in Asia and never really felt the urge to explore Europe until much later in her life, more the pity. She had felt an instant connection to Italy and loved every minute she spent there. It was the south she loved the most. The exciting energy of Naples and the sadness and deep beauty of Sicily. Even when she wasn't there, the sights, sounds, and memories haunted her thoughts, and she was sad until she could spend time there again. This visit was to see whether she could live there permanently. Whether she was able to sustain a simple, but not too frugal lifestyle. She was not even sure where she wanted to live. There was the rugged beauty of Scicli and it's surrounds. It's Baroque architecture and the desolate land high in the mountains, covered in moonscape clay pits and bushes of prickly pear. Then there was the mystery and energy of Palermo with it's sad, sad history of the mafia assassinations of judges, police, priests, and ordinary citizens who had become victims of those bloody massacres. Or maybe the vitality of seaside fishing villages with their tiny houses tucked close together, hugging the water's edge. How nice would it be to sit on your terrace looking out over the Mediterranean and experience all four seasons. Susan had only visited in the summer months and she was curious to know what it would be like to live there during winter or spring. For now, she was spending time surrounded by the beauty of Taormina. It was far too expensive to think of making a life for herself there, but it was wonderful to visit. Just to sit and absorb the atmosphere, browsing in the upmarket shops and eating in the wonderful restaurants. She was going to celebrate her seventieth birthday here....no, not celebrate, she would manage to get through the twenty-four hours, ticking over that milestone far away from family and friends, with a few drinks, a nice dinner, and a walk around the town. Welcome, seventy. Would things suddenly change? Would her face sink down and her energy levels drop? No, she laughed to herself. It just wasn't a very nice thought. The next stop would be eighty, if she was lucky enough to get that far. So she had come to Taormina, by herself, much to the consternation of her daughters. She would sit drinking prosecco, eating vongole, and looking out at the beautiful sea, and while she sat there alone, toasting her good health and happiness, the brilliant lights of Taormina and beyond, would stretch out along the coast like a necklace of precious jewels glittering there in front of her. She might shed a few tears, tears of happiness, tears for an unknown future, and tears because she didn't have anyone to share this moment with, only some harassed waiters and groups of noisy diners. Last night she had arrived at the chaotic bus terminus after a long journey from Catania. She had walked slowly, dragging her suitcase along the bumpy cobbled pathway to her B&B, Villa Nettuno. After registering at the reception desk, she had flopped on her bed and wondered what on earth she had done. Was she crazy? Anyway, it was too late now, here she was in Taormina and about to turn seventy. She had spent a few days at Villa Nettuno two years ago with two of her daughters and son-in-law. Susan liked its central location and the rooms were comfortable. The familiarity of the place also helped her feel less alone. I am happy here she thought and at least I know where I am.

The journey, her heightened emotions, and having had no dinner had caused her to spend a restless night, waking frequently in the middle of a series of very bizarre dreams. Now, this morning she had woken feeling depressed and heavy-headed. She knew that the only way she could sort herself out and lift this mood was to walk that feeling off, and maybe have a swim in the waters of the beautiful, clear Ionian Sea. After showering and having a quick breakfast of caffe latte and pastries on the terrace, Susan set off. She decided to catch the funicular down to the car park area and then make up her mind where she felt like going. There were many beaches around Taormina, places you could choose to suit your mood. The busy, endless rows of blue and white sun lounges and umbrellas lining the shore. The clink of glasses fizzing with Aperol Spritz and the air filled with the mouth-watering aroma of fritto misto or the deep garlicky smell of vongole. Or there was the walk over to Isola Bella. A mysterious island just a short distance from the coast. You could, at certain times, depending on the tides, walk across to the island. Buried amongst the trees and thick vegetation, was a building, a dark silent place, it's roof rising just above the tree line. Susan had heard it was possible to stay there. How you organised it she didn't know but it would probably be incredibly expensive. The island had also featured in the Italian TV drama, La Piovra, The Octopus. It had run for many years, the first few series having been filmed in locations around Palermo. A few episodes had also been shot in Taormina, in particular on Isola Bella. Susan had enjoyed watching the drama and remembered Isola Bella looking beautiful, but also slightly menacing. The family who were living in the house had links to the mafia and were being hunted down for their illegal banking practices, as well as other crimes.

Susan decided to walk out to Isola Bella, it suited her mood today, rather than the crowded bright, breezy resorts dotted along the coast. Isola Bella also had an impressive nature reserve which was protected by the World Wide Fund for Nature. The tiny island had been donated to the town of Taormina by Ferdinand I of Bourbon and later bought by Lady Florence Trevelyn. Susan had discovered on a previous visit that Lady Florence had also been responsible for building the dark mysterious villa, as well as planting a garden filled with exotic vegetation. It was the same Lady Florence who had designed the equally exotic, quirky gardens and built Villa Comunale in the town itself.

She should swim. She was sure it would help to clear her head and lift her mood. There weren't too many people about yet. Holidaymakers tended to have a bit of a lie-in and enjoy their breakfasts before heading out for the day, unless they had an early departure on one of the daily tours of the town and its surrounding districts. Susan gingerly felt her way along the dark, leafy pathway that twisted around the side of the rocky little island. She could see the roof of the mysterious villa from time to time, there slightly above the trees, watchful in the brooding silence. From time to time birds would suddenly rise up from the bushes, squawking loudly as if disturbed by something unseen. Susan could now see the sparkling water, and she headed towards it. Sometimes, an old statue would suddenly appear, it's moss covered face peering out of the greenery giving her a slight shock. The stoney stare seeming to follow her progress. At last, she reached the other side. Feeling sticky with sweat, her headache had steadily gotten worse. Susan couldn't wait to reach that cool water and immerse herself in it. She finally reached the shore and felt her way carefully through the clusters of rocks lying just under the water's surface.

Because the shore was so rocky, Susan had kept her rubber shoes on until she reached the sandy bottom, away from the rocks. The sudden coolness of the water tingled. Throwing her shoes back on to the shore she let herself sink into the refreshing sea. Floating on her back, Susan looked up at the bright blue sky. It was cloudless, and the day would become hotter, that was what you could expect in July. Day after day of blue skies, relentless sun, and very few clouds. There was a slight breeze that helped a little, but lying in the cool blue water, being rocked gently by the tiniest of waves, was all Susan desired. She stayed like that for maybe thirty minutes and then decided to swim a little way around the side of the island. Often there were small fishing boats or paddle boats that could be hired and taken out by sightseers to view the island and its surroundings, but it was still a little early for them. Ahead she could see a boat lying half out of the water, the submerged side was being tossed against the black glistening rocks that rose at the water's edge. Susan swam closer. She suddenly froze, staring ahead at what appeared to be an arm hanging out of the boat. Pushed by the waves, it flapped against the side limply. The boat looked old, definitely not a tourist boat, it also looked uncared for, with badly peeling red paint, and rust showing through on various parts of its body.

'Oh my God!' Susan gasped out loudly. Although she felt frightened, something kept pushing her forward. Her initial curiosity was gradually replaced by a compelling need to know more, no matter what it might turn out to be.

She could see now, as she moved closer, there was a complete body attached to that arm. He lay face upwards in the boat. It was the body of a young man, maybe late teens or early twenties. His face was frozen in an expression of surprise, his black hair was short and his vacant, dark brown eyes stared up at that relentless blue sky above. Despite the heat of the day he was wearing a dark jacket which was riddled with bullet holes. Susan could also see that under him and in the surrounding area were more bodies, maybe eight or nine. Women, men and children, their lifeless bodies rocking gently in the water that filled most of the boat. There appeared to be a multitude of bullet holes which had been sprayed relentlessly through the boat, tearing through bodies and leaving behind a carnage that seemed unbelievable in this atmosphere of stillness and beauty. It was like stepping into a scene of the worst type of horror film Susan could imagine. She gasped and started to cry loudly. She didn't know what to do, the shock of what lay in front of her finally sinking in. The water that not so long ago had been cool and refreshing, now felt icy and her body began to shake uncontrollably. The more she looked the more saddened she became.

Those poor, poor people. Who were they? Why were they here? From their skin and the clothes they wore, they were African, their thin smashed bodies now exposed to the elements. They had already started to become bloated and paler. It was too much to bear. Susan looked away, but there, further along, at the edge of the water, she could see more bodies wedged between rocks, the colors of their clothing merging with the sea, waving like so many flags against the rocky outcrops.

'What to do, what to do?' She groaned to herself. The initial shock turning into anger and despair. 'I'll have to call someone, the police?' She didn't even know where the police station was in Taormina, maybe the closest place would be Catania. Looking around Susan tried to see where she could best get out of the sea. Her shoes were back on the beach, which was now far behind her. Walking over those stones with bare feet was impossible. Her feet would be cut on those sharp, volcanic rocks. She had left her phone back in her room, so calling an emergency number was out of the question. She moved cautiously past the boat and its lifeless occupants. Up ahead Susan thought she could see a yellow patch of sand so she made slowly for that, if she could swim there she might be able to raise the alarm and get others to summon the police. She swam up on to the sand. Behind her, the boat lay silently, the waves lapping against its side. Looking back, it was now hard to imagine what she had just seen. Everything looked so peaceful. Susan got out of the water and checked where the nearest path was. It didn't take long for her to make a decision.

Just over a ridge of greenery, the sound of voices rose in the air. Italian voices arguing about something. Susan had been making a valiant attempt to learn Italian ever since she had fallen in love with the country. She could work out the gist of conversations, but anything a little more complicated was still beyond her expertise. This seemed to be about the behaviour of one of them at a party the night before and the voices were those of two young people. She saw them as she came up the path, they looked to be in their late twenties or early thirties. A girl, and a boy, in t-shirts and shorts, a backpack on the ground between them.

'I saw you looking at that German girl, go and find her if you want to be with her. I'm going back to Palermo. I can't stand it here anymore with you. I knew it was a mistake to come. I should have gone to Vito Lo Capo with the rest of the group. Just go Aurelio, just go!'

The girl stood, her hands in the air, her feet planted firmly in front of him and her face contorted with anger. She was about five foot six with strong muscled legs, and a slightly feline face. She had striking green eyes and high cheek bones. Her dark, thickly curled hair fell down over her shoulders. A white scarf, that looked to have designs of Indian gods printed on it, was tied loosely around her neck. The young man, to whom the attack was directed at, looked aggrieved. Tall and thin with several tattoos up and down his arms, his longish hair was caught up with a hair tie on top of his head.

'Angela, I didn't, you've got it all wrong!' he begged plaintively.

Susan came up behind them. 'Guys, guys,' she gasped. 'There's a boat down on the rocks behind us, there are lots of bodies in it, and a lot more along the shoreline. We need to tell someone. Do you know if there is a police station in Taormina?'

They both looked puzzled at first, a hysterical older woman suddenly appearing out of the bushes carrying on about bodies, was disconcerting to say the least, but after seeing that she was serious and not crazy, as far as they could tell, they quickly sprang into action.

'Yes, there is, there's one up on Corso Umberto,' the boy, Aurelio said. 'I'll go. I'll be quicker and I know where it is. You two better go back and wait with the boat in case people come along. I'll try and be as fast as I can.'

He seemed a cool sort of person and not particularly fazed by what she had just told him. Even better, he was ready to take charge. It was just that after overhearing a little of their passionate, emotional conversation, she was surprised by his quick, cool action.

He set off straight away, heading in the direction of the sandy pathway that led off the island to the mainland, where there was a beach resort. Susan knew he would then have to go up to the main road and try to get a lift into the town, it would take quite a while.

'We'd better go back,' Susan said. 'It's an awful sight, you'll need to prepare yourself,' and she turned back towards the way she had just come from.

They were still there. From a distance they looked like floating rubber beach toys, rocked gently by the waves. Angela stared ahead. 'Oddio,' she murmured, and quickly crossed herself.

Susan took a deep breath. 'We should wait up here and keep a lookout, there's no point going down into the water again. I have no idea how many bodies there are. They are around the side of the island as well. Many of them have become wedged in between the rocks.'

Angela looked thoughtful. 'Where do you think they came from?'

'They look like refugees,' Susan answered. 'Judging by what they're wearing, their features, and the type of boat they were in. I've seen pictures on the TV, and in newspapers, of migrants coming across the Mediterranean. I think they may have come across from one of the North African countries.'

'But why do you think they were murdered after they landed? I don't understand.'

'I have no idea either,' Susan said sadly. 'It's dreadful, when you think of the dangers they faced making a journey like that. They could have ended up dying in an accident at sea, drowning, or even captured by pirates. Then, after coming all this way and going through so much, to have reached their destination and finally thinking they were safe, they've ended up dead. Killed in such a ruthless way. It doesn't make any sense and it's heartbreaking.'

'We'll just have to wait for the police and see what happens from there, I suppose.' Susan stopped. 'Sorry, I am talking too much. It must be the shock. A delayed reaction.'

Angela stared ahead, sorrowfully.

They sat together for what seemed like hours, but was only a little over an hour, Susan worked out later. Perched on a rock, they kept a watchful eye on the devastating scene below. Angela had told Susan that she and Aurelio were in their final years at university in Palermo and were having a little break in Taormina. She was studying Italian literature and Aurelio, criminology. That must be why he had shown little shock at hearing Susan describe the scene, he had probably studied more macabre crimes than Susan had ever heard of.

The sound of voices was now audible through the dense trees and bushes, and before long the owners of those voices appeared. There were three of them, along with Aurelio. Two of them wore the uniforms of the Polizia di Stato, the other was plain-clothed. The man in plainclothes was obviously in charge. He looked at Susan with a questioning look. 'Are you the one who found them?'

His English was clear, with little accent.

'Yes I did. There are so many of them, shot, in the boat and along the shoreline of the island.' Her eyes filled with tears and she was suddenly quiet. Beads of sweat broke out on her forehead and upper lip. Angela took hold of Susan's hand and patted it gently. 'It's alright, take a deep breath, you'll be ok. I've got water in the backpack, hold on I'll get it.' Gratefully, Susan took the water and drank some. Almost immediately she started feeling better. The denseness of the vegetation hadn't helped either, it was making her feel claustrophobic. An oppressive, airless atmosphere and the thought of what lay below made her feel sick and anxious.

'Thank you, Angela. I'm feeling much better now.'

The plain-clothed policeman signalled to the uniformed men to follow him down to the water. Angela, still holding Susan's hand, and Aurelio, followed slowly behind.

There was a sudden gasp from one of the uniforms as they stood looking at the shocking sight in front of them.

'Oddio!' The inspector said softly to himself. 'We'd better call Dr. Russo and the forensic team out here, we'll need to transport the bodies too. It will have to be the government hospital in Catania, we don't have any room here. Call Lo Bianco at Headquarters in Catania too… and the Coast Guard as well. This is massive, a real headache, and right here on our doorstep.' He shook his head in disbelief.

'Who on earth is responsible for this massacre? It's unwarranted and vicious, completely shocking,' he continued.

'I can see children down there too. Who would do such a thing?'

His soft brown eyes were full of shock and sadness. They all stood silently, taking in the terrible scene. 'May God have mercy on them, poor devils.'

He turned back to Susan and Angela. 'Sorry, this terrible business has made me forget my manners. I'm Commissario Luca Lombardo, and you are?'

'Susan Blackstone, from Australia,' she added, as she shook his extended hand. 'I'm on holiday here.' You're babbling, Susan thought to herself. Calm down. Taking a deep breath, she continued with her story.

'I was having a swim this morning around eight-thirty, and came across them, there are more around the side. There look to be around thirty, or maybe even more, it's so shocking, I still can't get my head around it. Do you think they are refugees? I just thought, after seeing what they are wearing, and the type of boat and….' she stopped talking. 'Sorry, I'm rattling on, it's the shock I think, and having to look at them again.'

'Of course I don't like to make assumptions, but certainly at first glance, it does look like it. We'll have to wait though, until the experts get here, before we can have any real idea or understanding of what happened down there…'

Angela then gave him details of who she was and how she had ended up here with Susan. The commissario had met her father, a well-known businessman and banker from Palermo, several times, and he seemed satisfied with their brief statements, for now.

While he was giving his men orders and speaking on the phone to various people, Susan took the opportunity to take a closer look at him. Quite tall for a southern Italian, he was gangly and looked a little awkward in this setting. His summer weight jacket hung loosely, off shoulders which were slightly hunched. He had brownish, grey flecked hair which was a little long and disheveled in the heat. A small trim moustache sat neatly above a gently smiling mouth. His eyes were deep brown and kind, but at the same time, keenly observant. There was a gentle firmness about him. A man who was used to giving orders and being obeyed. Susan had the feeling he had travelled or studied abroad in an English speaking country as he spoke with confidence and ease. She felt comfortable in his presence and knew that he was a man who would get the job done. Despite his relaxed manner, there was nothing easygoing about him though. I can't imagine he would suffer fools or laziness, Susan thought to herself.

'Where are you staying, Signora Susan?' Commissario Lombardo asked.

'At Villa Nettuno.'

'I'll need to speak to you again at some point. Do you have any plans over the next day or two?'

'No, I'll be here in Taormina, but I'm meant be going back to Cava D'Aliga in three days.'

'Oh, it will be before then, probably tomorrow. You can both go now,' and he turned and went back to his investigation. It was going to be a long, long day.

Susan and Angela started to walk slowly back, there was no sign of Aurelio, he must have followed the uniforms down to the water. It would be a great opportunity for the criminology student, Susan couldn't help thinking.

Chapter 3

After the two women had left, Commissario Lombardo walked down to meet the other officers. They had already begun a preliminary inspection of what lay before them. The two men looked visibly shocked. There was non of the light-hearted banter the Commissario and his men sometimes engaged in to try to lighten the mood of some of the crime scenes they were called to. This time the three of them, with Aurelio watching from the sidelines, walked silently between the bodies they could reach, looking but not touching anything. That would be the job of the forensic team when they arrived. The others would have to be taken from the water using the police launch which was due any minute.

'This is unbelievable, it's like something from an apocalyptic movie,' one of the uniforms muttered.

'I know, Roberto, I've never seen anything on this scale, even the terrible train derailment that happened a couple of years ago when I was stationed in Calabria, was nothing like this. The awful thing is that someone, or a group of people, more likely a group, if you look at the extent of the carnage, is responsible for this. I find it hard to believe that something of this magnitude could have been done by only one person.'

One of the officers spoke up, 'I agree boss, I think for this to have been done by just one person would be pretty difficult. I'd say we are looking at the work of a group too, maybe three or possibly four people using semi-automatic weapons, and fired at fairly close range. Those poor devils would have had to look their assailants in the eyes, those of them who knew what was coming, that is. It's barbaric and senseless.'

Everyone was silent for a moment, Lombardo felt anger stirring in him. The longer he looked at the bloody scene in front of him, the angrier he felt. 'I'll get the bastards who did this, don't you worry,' he spoke softly as he made a promise to those poor broken bodies floating in the sea.

Police officers from other areas started to arrive, plus the forensic teams. It was a difficult job, there were so many bodies and each one had to be examined and at the same time treated with dignity. Every officer's face bore a look of shock and anger as they went about their jobs quietly. Before too long the sound of a motorboat was heard, it's siren on full blast. Around the corner of the island came the coast guard from Catania. Lo Bianco was standing at the front of the boat and waved as he caught sight of Lombardo. When the boat drew closer to the shore he called out to him. 'What on earth has been going on in your neck of the woods, it looks like a blood bath?'

'Yes, it's pretty terrible, prepare yourself for a bad one, and we haven't a clue why this has happened.' Lombardo shouted back as the boat drew into the side of the island... 'Oddio! What a bloody disaster...looks like a hell of a lot of work has to be done. I don't know that we have the resources in Catania. Should we think about letting them know in Palermo, we might need to use their facilities. Taking the bodies to Catania might put too much of a strain on the hospital there,' he added, hesitantly.

'I don't really want to involve the chief in Palermo, unless I have to,' Lombardo answered. 'There have been some strange things happening there lately. Evidence going missing, known criminals being allowed out on bail and suddenly turning up in Malta. I want to try and keep everything down here rather than letting the powers that be in on this. Let's just see what we can find out first before we let them know. As it is, I bet the first thing they do when they find out what has happened will be to either wash their hands of it, or try and take over to manipulate the evidence. It depends on who they think might be involved. I'd rather do as much as we can, before anything can be corrupted. Can you understand my reluctance, Lo Bianco? It's sometimes hard to know who to trust. We've been colleagues for a long time now, and I think we understand each other. I'm only on a short term secondment down here, helping them out with the tourism extortion case. I have to go back to Palermo soon, but if we can just keep the preliminary investigation down here while I'm in charge. After I return to Palermo I'll already have control of the investigation so it would be harder to cover things up then.' Lo Bianco nodded his head slowly, musing on what Lombardo had just said.

'Yes ok, we'll try and do as much as we can before we get stopped, or the case gets taken over. Let's hope it stays with you.'

He could understand Lombardo's reluctance to hand over too much responsibility to the Questura, Police Headquarters, in Palermo. During the nineties there had been a spate of assassinations, of police, judges, and even priests. In fact, anyone who dared to speak out against mafia complicity and intimidation in and around that city. Lombardo's uncle had been a decorated police officer, much loved by the people of Palermo for his work with disadvantaged children.

He had waged a constant battle against the hardship the mafia imposed on the lives of Palermo citizens, with their menacing threats, and the unceasing demands for *pizzo*, the payment of protection money.

He had been part of a detail escorting a well-known judge on his way to hear evidence against one of the mafia bosses. The convoy of four cars had been ambushed and the occupants mown down in a hail of bullets, fired by a group of eight men, hidden at the side of the road. All died, including Lombardo's beloved uncle. That moment had shaped his future, his choice of profession, his hatred of corruption, and his relentless fight to make sure his uncle's death had not been in vain. He would never forget those in the Polizia di Stato, the State Police Force, from Palermo who had melted into the background, too scared to speak out and too scared to stand beside him, his aunt and the rest of his family in their hour of need. Whenever he had doubts about why he was doing what he did, and felt the whole thing was pointless, he remembered that day, and his doubts were immediately replaced with a strong determination to win.

His relationship with the State Police Force was an uneasy one at the best of times, but over the last couple of years' things had got decidedly worse. He'd made several complaints about one of the chiefs and his treatment of refugees, especially women, and had suddenly found himself transferred to the wilds of Calabria as a liaison officer. While he was there, he had to deal with a terrible train accident. It was during that time he realised that he didn't belong there, in fact, his presence was more of an embarrassment than a help. It was obvious his fellow officers felt awkward around him. He wasn't Calabrian, he was Sicilian. It was no secret that he had been sent there as punishment for critisising those in power, as well as being a stirrer, under the pretext of cross border cooperation. After he felt he'd been banished for long enough, he requested a transfer back to Palermo for humanitarian reasons. His aunt was getting older and he needed to be close to her. He had been back for less than six months, when he became the lead investigator on a dreadful organ trafficking case. During that time, he had again managed to tread on the toes of some very powerful people who didn't want a spotlight shone on some of their more dubious connections...

At the conclusion of the case, and most of the middlemen jailed, there had been another change for Lombardo. He now spent much of his time in Taormina, on assignment. A job gifted to him by headquarters, under the guise of overseeing a task force set up to deal with problems relating to the mafia infiltration of the tourism business. He was meant to be taking a rest from fieldwork. His main duty at the moment, consisted of the issuing orders of jobs others had to do. But today, things had suddenly changed.

The mafia control was penetrating anything related to tourism in this very wealthy tourist town. Boat rentals, tours, and other tourist-related businesses were caught up in the mafia's strangling tentacles, which had wound themselves around the most ordinary of pastimes. As well as money-making enterprises, these also doubled as money laundering schemes. Two families were responsible for these illegal activities. They had once been bitter enemies but a gradual takeover of many of their previous businesses by the Southern Italian ndrangheta had led them to join forces and look for greener pastures in their local areas. Lombardo was meant to deal mainly with the cumbersome bureaucratic red tape coming out of Palermo and further afield from Rome. He was also responsible for the overall supervision of the team of young recruits working at Taormina headquarters. This posting was meant to be a reward. The promise of a less stressful recovery period after an intense and incredibly traumatic year on the front line working to expose, and bring to justice, a people-trafficking ring which was also linked to the trade in human organs. This had almost been the end of him. He had, with his team, raided and rescued thirty refugee children of varying ages, from a house on the coast, near the seaside village of Santa Flavia. It had challenged his belief in good, and after it was over he had seriously considered leaving the police force. He had lost all faith in human kindness. His long term relationship had crumbled under the stress, long hours, and the emotional toll that the case had taken on him. If he wanted to be cynical, he also knew that this posting was also a way of keeping him away from headquarters. Too many people had been caught up in this investigation, and there were a few politicians who had rapidly left for long holidays in Costa Rica and Bulgaria.

Now, any free time he had was spent helping out at his uncle's refuge, playing football with disadvantaged kids, including the new arrivals. The refugees, and the migrants tossed up on the shores and in the camps around Palermo and Catania and the other smaller towns further away. Father Benedict, was the brother of the murdered police officer. Like Lombardo he had also been deeply affected by his death and joined the priesthood. He now devoted his life to working with these refugees as well as the forgotten, the disadvantaged, and the exploited in the poor districts and surrounding villages of Palermo.

Over the last couple of months, Lombardo had begun to feel stronger and more positive about his job as a policeman. Taormina had given him a chance to step back and not be at the forefront of an investigation. But now, with this discovery of the forty migrants massacred in the sea, beside an idyllic, mysterious island, his reasonably peaceful life had been severely disrupted. He took a deep breath and went back to look at how things were progressing with the collection and transporting of the bodies back to Catania.

Chapter 4

After walking off the island and up to the main road, Susan and Angela parted ways. Angela and Aurelio were staying in a backpacker place just off the main road. Susan continued on to the bus depot and car park, then caught the funicular up to the main town. It was already crowded with tourists walking to the various attractions in the historically beautiful town, their maps, guidebooks and cameras at the ready. Susan decided to stop off at a little coffee bar and have a pastry and espresso. After everything that had gone on she now felt a sudden tiredness, a shot of coffee and some sugar was what she needed. It was now after ten-thirty but felt much later. She ordered and then found a place outside to sit, well away from the large noisy groups inside.

Susan started to go over the events of the morning in her head. Although the initial shock had worn off she still felt an extreme sadness punctuated now and then with bursts of anger. Why do that to those poor, poor people, it seemed so senseless. She hoped they would get to the bottom of it and make the people responsible pay dearly for what they had done. After finishing her coffee Susan decided to walk around to the beautiful gardens of Villa Comunale, she always felt a sense of peace when she was there. The quirky buildings and sculptures erected in the various nooks and crannies made her smile. Susan also found its history fascinating. The villa and gardens had originally been owned by a Scottish noblewoman, Lady Florence Trevelyn. The same Lady Florence who was connected to Isola Bella. She had left her country as a result of a scandal. She had had an affair with the heir to the British throne, Edward VII, which unsurprisingly caused a few problems, so she had set off for Italy, which seemed the best thing to do under the circumstances. After arriving in Taormina she married Mayor Prof. Salvatore Cacciola. The garden became the property of the town in nineteen twenty-two. Lady Trevelyan's buildings, known as follies are dotted around the garden. Walking through soft green paths, broken here and there with large bursts of color from bright purple bougainvillea and huge magnolias, Susan slowly regained her sense of normality. The coffee had cleared her head and she was able to think a bit more clearly and rationally. Walking to the edge of the garden Susan looked down over the long, low, wall. The buildings directly below, and the sea beyond, were set out in a huge panoramic vista, spreading out then melting away into a far off, hazy horizon. She could see Giardini Naxos and the railway station, the tiny figures of travellers hurrying to catch their trains. Boats bobbed in the water, small brightly coloured fishing boats, beautiful, luxurious pleasure cruisers, small motorboats roaring far out from the shore, and tall, elegant yachts, their sails moving gently in the light offshore breeze. Out of the corner of her eye, she saw police boats heading off in the direction of Isola Bella. She counted at least four, some were coming from further away, probably Catania.

Susan decided to walk back to Villa Nettuno and have a rest, the day was heating up and the crowds were becoming increasingly dense. In another hour most of the shops would shut for the afternoon siesta, not opening again until around five. People tended to get in a bit of must-do shopping before this happened. Passing under the archway and turning the corner, Susan could see her B&B up ahead. Buses were pulling in near the flight of steps leading up to the small hotel. Passengers, getting down, then going their separate ways to the various parts of town and beyond. The hotel was quiet. Beautifully decorated rooms led off from the main foyer. A statue of the god Nettuno or Neptune took pride of place on the terrace ahead. A few guests sat outside enjoying the coolness of the garden, making plans for the days ahead. Susan took her room key from Salvo who was doing morning reception duty. Salvo was the son of the owners Guiseppina and Raffaele.

'Morning Salvo, how is everything?' Susan asked.

'Terrible, so terrible, have you heard about the bodies they found near Isola Bella, Signora Susan?' Was his passionate reply.

'Oh yes, I did,' she answered. 'I heard people talking about it when I stopped for a coffee.' She didn't feel like telling him she was the one who had found them. 'I suppose there will be lots of police around the town...'

'Yes, and reporters too... who could have done this and why?'

'I think that is a question everyone will be asking. It seems such a cruel and senseless thing to do.' She left him there, still talking with some other guests who had just come in.

After saying goodbye, she turned and went down the corridor. She knew this would be one of the main topics of conversation taking place in Taormina right now. Everyone would have an opinion and the gossip and speculation would last until the crime had been solved. To top it off it was the peak of the tourist season.

Her room was quiet and cool. She lay down on her bed in utter relief and shut her eyes. However, no sooner had they closed, visions of floating bodies filled her thoughts. Small children huddled under their parents, the first boy she had seen, his arm-flapping carelessly over the side of the boat, like a piece of discarded rubbish... flotsam and jetsam... the phrase came to mind again.

She must have fallen asleep. The sound of loud voices outside her room awakened her with a jolt, parts of a leftover dream still lingering in her mind. It took some moments before she came slowly back to the present, and her surroundings. There was a deep sense of sadness and foreboding which hung over her like a heavy cloud just before a downpour. The room was close and warm, so she quickly got off the bed and opened the door which led out to a small terrace. As the cool air entered the room, the voices moved on and gradually faded away.

Once again, thoughts of the bodies on the boat reentered her mind. She wondered how the commissario and his men were doing. She hoped they had been able to take the bodies away quickly, to a place where they could lie quietly, away from the indignity of being on display, their dreadful wounds, their faces forever frozen in shocked expressions at their violent, senseless deaths. Her thoughts then wandered back to the commissario. He was certainly an attractive man and from the way he had reacted to the violent crime scene she felt there was a gentle, compassionate side to him as well. Spending more time with him would not be difficult, in fact she was rather looking forward to their next meeting. I wonder if there is a Signora Lombardo? She smiled to herself. It might be nice to get to know him a little better, she thought and reluctantly let go of her daydream.

A quick glance at the clock by her bed jolted her out of her pleasant thoughts, it was almost five o'clock, she had slept for nearly four hours. After taking a shower and putting on the new white dress she had bought especially for this holiday, her mood lifted. The soft fabric fell around her skin and she felt comfortable and much cooler. The face that stared back at her from the mirror near the door, now looked less stressed. The dark shadows under her eyes had gone and the lines had softened. Her thick ash coloured hair was caught up in a bright scarf on top of her head. The overall effect was of a relaxed, confident woman on her way out for a pleasant evening. I think I'll go and sit in Piazza Duomo, have an aperitivo, and do a little people watching, Susan thought. She gathered up her bag and a shawl and left the room. Salvo was still on reception, 'ciao Susanna,' he said brightly, taking her room key and putting it in her pigeon hole.

'Hi Salvo, busy?'

'Aah! Always busy, always tired!' he answered with a feigned expression of exhaustion. Susan smiled, Salvo would never be exhausted from working, partying maybe, but not working. He was the beloved youngest son. His days on the reception desk were spent talking to friends, drinking numerous espressos, and flirting with women of any age who were staying at the B&B..... tired from working....she laughed.

'Have a nice evening Susanna,' he called after her. 'Grazie Salvo, you too,' and she headed out the door, down the steps, and into the cool evening air. The lights were just coming on and the cobbled footpaths were becoming more crowded with people starting to take the evening promenade, *una passeggiata*, along Corso Umberto. There were tourists from all over the world and whilst they might have been speaking in different languages, they were all enjoying the breathtaking beauty of

Taormina. Susan passed boutiques full of clothing she could never afford and shops crammed with souvenirs made in China. Godfather t-shirts flapped on their hooks and caps and coasters filled shelf after shelf. Most of these souvenir shops were operated by migrants and did a roaring trade.

Little trattorias were starting to open, tables were being laid and staff were gearing up for the long night ahead. It's my birthday tomorrow, she suddenly thought. How strange, I haven't thought about it once today, and she walked on with a lighter step. Sudden, horrendous events, did have a way of making everything else pale into insignificance.

She stopped at Albertinos, a small but incredibly popular trattoria where rows of tables were placed up and down the steps. They were beautifully patterned with lots of colored local tiles, the motifs and color choices so typically Sicilian. Deep blues like the sea and sky, bright yellow like the sun and lemons and green like the vineyards and olive groves. Marco, one of the waiters called out to her. 'Ciao Susan. How are you?'

'Great, Marco. I'm really good.' she sat down at one of the small tables.

'What will you have, an Aperol Spritz? Some antipasti?'

'Yes, that sounds good,' she smiled. Marco hurried off, and Susan sat looking around her. The tables were starting to fill up. People dressed for early evening, brightly patterned patio wear was favoured by the women, with bejewelled sandals that tapped and sparkled on the terracotta tiles. Their tanned healthy skin glowed in the late afternoon sun.

The men wore open-necked shirts made from beautiful soft linen, matched with casual trousers and open sandals. Many of them had dark unshaven faces with soft brown eyes and full generous mouths. They smiled and laughed amongst themselves, the beautiful people of Taormina. For many years the rich and famous had lived here. Actors, writers and painters had been inspired by the ancient buildings, the rugged beauty of its landscape and the dark brooding volcanic rock on which it was built. Just sitting there filled Susan with joy, being in one of the most beautiful places she had ever spent time in.

'Here you are.' Marco was back with her drink and a platter of antipasti. Salty olives, tiny arancini, pieces of toasted bread topped with chopped tomato and basil, a shiny ball of buffalo mozzarella, and crisp salty grisini.

For a while, Susan focused on her drink and eating the tasty morsels, but suddenly her thoughts were disrupted by the sound of a heated argument at a table nearby. Two men, who looked Sicilian, were engaged in a conversation with another man who looked African.

From Susan's limited understanding of Italian, it was something to do with money, a payment hadn't been received by the African and the Sicilians didn't think they should pay. Voices rose louder, the African stood over the other two, pleading for some sort of payment. The Sicilians then got up from the table, pushed past him and walked down the steps. The African stared after them in disbelief, then slowly walked away too, his feet dragging dejectedly along the pebbled pathway.

What had that been about? Susan wondered. She felt a bit sorry for the African, he seemed distressed and confused judging by the tone of his pleading voice. Well, I hope they work it out, she thought and went back to her drink.

'Good evening Signora Susan,' a voice came from behind her.

'Oh, Commissario, it's you. How are you? Have you finished dealing with things?' She asked, slightly flustered by his sudden appearance.

'For the moment, but with a case like this you never really stop until the guilty have been brought to justice,' he answered with a sigh. 'It was very confronting for every-one involved, but we managed to get all the bodies taken to Catania. There were thirty-five altogether, men, women, and children, so, so sad and unwarranted. The faces I saw, as we pulled those people out of the sea will haunt me for a long time to come. Poor poor people,' he said again. 'No one deserves to end up like that. Now we have to try and work out who did this and why.'

'Would you like to join me?' Susan suddenly asked, amazed at this sudden burst of courage, it was probably the wine, the aperitivo, the beautiful evening......

'Oh, I'm sorry, another time, for sure. I'm just on my way back to headquarters to start writing the report on what hap-pened. I also have to start looking into information we have on known people smugglers in the area or anyone who might be able to help us with our inquiries. I was wondering if you could call into headquarters tomorrow morning so that we can take your statement.'

'Of course, I would be happy to. I hope this terrible crime is solved as quickly as possible. I'm not sure where the police sta-tion is, but I'll ask, and get someone to show me the way.'

'Here's my card, it has a small map on the back.'

'Ok, I'll see you tomorrow then.'

'Enjoy the rest of your evening.'

Susan watched as he walked back down the steps. He was so calm, you couldn't help but feel safe around him, and attractive too.

'Do you know the Commissario?' Marco came up to her, a questioning look on his face. 'Nothing bad has happened, I hope?'

'No nothing like that, I just got involved in something the police are investigating and he needed me to go over some of the facts. It's ok Marco, don't worry. What's good on the menu today? I might have my primo platti now.'

'How about some vongole, the clams are fresh from the sea and there is some beautiful swordfish to follow.'

'That sounds wonderful, yes, that will be perfect.'

As usual, the food was delicious. The vongole, garlicky, with the right amount of lemon and parsley and the swordfish to die for. Freshly caught, with just a light seasoning of salt and pepper, lemon and a sprinkling of finely chopped parsley. It was served with small potatoes and a salade verde. After the meal and two glasses of dry white wine, it was time to walk back to the B&B. She would take the long way back, the food and wine had made her a little sleepy and she wanted to clear her head before jotting down some notes about this morning. They might help me to remember things ready for the meeting with the Commissario tomorrow, Susan thought.

As she made her way back to the hotel, the restaurants and bars were in full swing, the atmosphere was light and carefree, as it should be during holiday season in a holiday town.

She had almost reached the steps leading up to Villa Nettuno, when in the distance, near the beginning of the funicular, she saw a group of people shouting and gesturing at something on the ground. As she moved closer, she could see someone sprawled on the cobblestones, surrounded by people, several of whom were kneeling in front of the person. She caught a glimpse of the clothing and then moved a little closer, looking beyond the body to the face, which gazed with sightless eyes, at the stary sky above. A trickle of blood ran from the corner of his mouth, a larger amount pooling into a red stain on the front of his shirt. A knife handle protruded from the centre of the patch. Susan gasped, it was the African she had seen earlier, arguing with the Sicilians in Albertino's trattoria.

Chapter 5

Commissario Luca Lombardo had just arrived back at headquarters, determined to make a start on his report. He was still disturbed and puzzled by the events of the day. The faces of the people he had seen in the water around Isola Bella were still fresh in his mind, and he was having difficulty coming to terms with the terrible brutality and lack of compassion evident in that crime. He had never seen anything like it in his nearly thirty years in the Polizia di Stato. He had seen some pretty horrific crimes especially during his time in Calabria but at least you knew the reasons why, greed, vendettas, jealousy and power came to mind, but at the moment this particular crime seemed completely senseless. Why kill these refugees when they had already paid their money and managed to make the journey safely out of the waters of North Africa and into the Mediterranean Sea? It was certainly strange.

'Commissario, Commissario,' a desperate voice came from the passageway outside his office. 'What is it Gianluca?' he replied to his Sergeant's urgent call.

'Someone's been found dead near the funicular ticket box!'

'Is anyone there already?' Lombardo asked.

'A couple of officers who were on patrol just called it in. An African with a stab wound to his chest, he couldn't be revived and died at the scene.'

'Ok, let's go, have you called forensics?' he asked. 'This is getting to be a habit I could do without,' he sighed.

'Yes, already,' Gianluca answered. Lombardo got up from his desk, the paperwork would have to wait for another time. This relatively crime-free town was starting to resemble the back streets of Palermo, he thought, as he followed Gianluca out to the police car.

When they pulled up, there was quite a crowd around the body, people were closing in around it, gesturing and making a huge fuss. The two officers were doing a poor job of holding them back. Lombardo and Gianluca pushed their way through and looked at the body on the ground. Someone had covered the face with a t-shirt, the red stain, a burst of bright color against the original pale patterned shirt. The handle of a knife stuck out from the center of the bloody patch.

Lombardo pulled away the t-shirt and started into the dead eyes of the African. He looked to be between thirty and forty and painfully thin. His ragged trousers were torn and frayed at the seams, his shirt, what could be seen of it under the bloodstains, was washed to the point of being threadbare. His scuffed sandals lay a little way from his calloused feet.

'What on earth has gone on here? This seems very much out of the ordinary,' Lombardo murmured to Gianluca. There weren't that many refugees around here, just the usual ones near the bus depots, and the sellers who walked up and down the beaches offering strange trinkets, blankets, and cheap toys to the sunbathers baking on their sunlounges.

He quickly scanned the crowd, looking for anything out of the ordinary. There was a familiar face, standing back from the crowd, it was Susan... 'Signora Susan!' He moved quickly towards her, 'what are you doing here?'

'Commissario, thank goodness you're here! I was on my way back to the hotel and noticed a crowd, I came over and saw this poor man lying on the ground.'

Her face was pale and she looked shocked. He gently led her away from the crowd and up the steps into the foyer of the hotel. 'Let's just sit for a minute,' he said, moving into the guest sitting room, off to the side of the lobby.

'I've seen that man before,' Susan said. 'While I was having dinner. It must have been just after you left. He was arguing with two Sicilians, I could only understand a little, it was something about money. Sorry, my Italian is not so good and my Sicilian is non-existant. When he left, he looked very dejected, but also angry, and now he is dead! What a day! what else can happen?'

'What did the two men he was arguing with look like?'

'One was short and fat, and wore a lot of gold jewellery. The other was taller and slimmer, with a thin moustache, he was almost bald and had cruel dark eyes. I could never forget those eyes. In fact, I remember thinking to myself, I wouldn't want to mess with him, he looked capable of anything.'

'I'm sorry to do this, especially with what you've been through today, but I need you to come to the Questura, the police station, and look at some photographs. We should do it as soon as possible, while those faces are still fresh in your memory. You never know, you might just recognise one of the faces you saw.'

'Well, they're certainly two faces I won't forget in a hurry.'

Susan slowly got up from the couch and braced herself for what she knew would be a daunting task. 'Ok, I'm ready, let's go.'

They walked down the steps and on to the footpath. She could see the police team still working, and the crowd milling around at the edges. 'My car's just over there.' Lombardo pointed to a dusty looking blue hatchback parked on the other side of the road. Susan got in and they sped off down the road towards the Questura. She could see patches of lights beyond the trees on the side of the road. They must be from ships moored down in the harbor at Giardini Naxos she thought absently. In what seemed like a matter of moments they pulled up outside the police station. It looked like a normal office building except for the discreet brass nameplate outside, Questura di Taormina. Lombardo opened the door for her and they went quickly up the steps and into a chaotic reception area. A harrassed looking uniformed policeman was surrounded by a group of at least ten people all shouting and gesturing at him. He was trying to help, but seemed powerless to bring any order to the unruly throng. In a corner by a door, a man sat nursing his head, there was a huge gash above his right eye. Lombardo pushed past them, ignoring the noise and chaos, and headed for an office further down the corridor and away from the madness. Susan followed closely behind, not daring to lose sight of him. At last, they reached the relative quietness of the office. The continuing din could be heard in the distance but it was a minor distraction now. Lombardo picked up the phone and asked someone to bring some files of mug shots for Susan to look at. Hopefully, she might recognise the men she had seen earlier in the trattoria. A young man in uniform knocked, then walked in carrying a pile of folders. 'Grazie, Tony,' Lombardo called after him as he left the room. He opened the first folder and placed it in front of her. A series of faces stared up at her, fat, grizzly faces, thin faces with shifty eyes, handsome ones, sad ones, careworn, aggressive.... on they went page after page, a procession of faces that had come into contact with the law, for any number of reasons. They were halfway through the fourth file when a familiar face looked back at her, it was one of the men from the trattoria. 'There's one!' Susan exclaimed.

'Now, who is this?' Lombardo looked carefully at the information listed below the photo of a particularly nasty looking character. 'Aaah... Bonfiglio, Gianni, age fifty-three, from Palermo. He's what's called a standover man, a collector of gambling debts as well as other types of debts. How interesting, according to this file he works for a particular family, the Saconne family, and, surprise, surprise, he has several priors, all related to extortion with menace. I wonder what his connection is to that poor dead African?' Lombardo spoke, almost to himself, as he took out the photo making a note of the details, then got Susan to start turning the pages again. It had been another hour and another three files when there was another familiar face. It was the other man, a little younger, but definitely the same one.

'That's the other one!' Susan sighed with relief. This was all getting a bit much. It was exhausting work looking at all those faces.

'Costa, Tony, that makes sense, he's an associate of Bonfiglio's and also works for the Saconne family.' The Commissario looked pleased with the results.

Thank goodness she could stop now, she didn't know how much longer she could have kept it up. Looking at page after page of the faces of criminals left her feeling helpless and depressed. Were there that many lawbreakers in this small area of Sicily? She was just about to close the file when another familiar face stared up at her, it was Aurelio. 'Goodness, isn't that Aurelio?'

'Haha no!' Lombardo said, laughing. 'It's his cousin, Guiseppi, their fathers are brothers. Guiseppi, or Peppino as everyone calls him, is the son and heir of Don Vicenzu Saconne. Those two men you have identified work for them. Peppino is someone who has been involved in many shady dealings, but it's been hard to connect him legally to any of them. He's a real slippery customer. Aurelio's father is the opposite, he is the chairman of several groups that help refugees, you could not get two brothers less alike than those two. Guiseppi is an unstable person with a drug problem. He has been in trouble a quite few times, although his father tries to keep him on a short leash by putting him in charge of several of his businesses that are low profile. He also has a very short temper and has been involved in some nasty incidents including the intimidation of migrants who won't hand over protection money from their already struggling businesses. He was also linked to the death of a young girl last year. She was severely beaten and left to die in the public gardens in Palermo. It was a terrible thing. We thought he had had something to do with it, but several people gave him a cast-iron alibi, and so nothing ever came of it. But we are watching, we'll never let it rest, and one day he will trip up and we will be waiting to catch him.' Lombardo looked even more determined, as he finished describing Aurelio's cousin.

'But Aurelio is studying criminology, isn't he? What a strange family, both on different sides of the law. I wonder what would happen if there came a time when they had to choose between family and what is right?'

'Yes, I'm sure there will be a time and it is probably closer than you might think. There have been several incidents during the last year where the business interests of Guiseppi's father, Don S., were encroaching on Aurelio's father's charitable organisations. Sooner or later, and I tend to think sooner, there will be a clash and then we will see what the fallout will be.

At least we have a lead now, those two faces you have identified will hopefully give us a lead to follow. I am truly grateful that you were able to help.'

'Me too,' Susan replied.

'I'll get someone to drive you back to Villa Nettuno now.' Commissario Lombardo got up from his seat and Susan got up too. They both walked out together, glad that some progress had been made at last. The reception area was quieter now, the rowdy group had gone, as had the man who had been slumped in the corner. They had been replaced by two distraught elderly people who had been the victims of a pickpocket.

'Unfortunately, this is very common at this time of year,' Lombardo commented. 'Taormina is rich pickings for petty thieves, and some not so petty. They come from everywhere, even as far as Naples. It's our busiest time of year, and now we have the added burden of these extra crimes. The senseless deaths of those poor souls in the sea and now a dead African. We might have to call for some reinforcements, if things get any worse.'

They reached the entrance, where a police car was waiting near the steps.

'Thanks again for your help,' he said, as he held the rear door open for Susan. 'I'll be in touch.'

The car drove off and Susan slumped into the worn leather of the seat. She felt exhausted. What a day! Her emotions were raw and the tiredness seemed to make everything worse. She was so far away from her children, and not for the first time she wondered what on earth she was doing here, and now she was caught up in something decidedly nasty, and probably dangerous. Maybe I should just get on a plane and leave she thought...

It's probably the exhaustion making me think like that. I'll see how I feel tomorrow and then decide what to do. She was meant to be going back to Cava D'Aliga in three days, what if she had to stay on here? She'd speak about it with Commissario Lombardo tomorrow, at least he was nice, in fact he was more than nice, Susan smiled to herself. Despite the hideous situation she was in, there were some advantages.

Susan walked wearily to the top of the steps of Villa Nettuno and pushed open the door. She was surprised it wasn't locked, as it was now past midnight. Usually you had to ring a bell and someone would unlock the door.

'Buono notte,' a voice greeted her. It was Aurelio looking very chummy with the guy on the reception desk.

'Oh, hi Aurelio, what are you doing here?'

'Actually, waiting for you,' he smiled back at her.

'I've been at the Questura with Commissario Lombardo. Did you know about the African who was killed down the street near the bus depot? I saw two men arguing with him when I was having dinner, so I had to go and look through files of mug shots with the commissario.'

'Ah, yes, I arrived just as they were taking away the body. I wondered what had happened? It looked pretty disturbing.'

'Yes it was, very…. Anyway, what was it you wanted to see me about Aurelio, it's late, is everything alright?'

'Have you seen Angela? We'd made a plan to meet up for dinner at around nine, but she didn't turn up or message me or anything, it's so unlike her. I thought she might have called in to see you. She mentioned wanting to talk to you about something she had thought of when we were on Isola Bella. I think it had something to do with the people in the boat. Now I can't find her anywhere. I've been back to where we were staying and they hadn't seen her since about three. I went with the police to

Catania when they brought the bodies back there. I wanted to look at some things and talk to a few people. I thought it might help me with the thesis I'm writing. That's why we made the plan to meet later. It's so not like her. If she says she's going to be somewhere, she always turns up, or at least lets you know if she can't make it.' He looked so confused and upset at being stood up, Susan couldn't help but feel sorry for him.

'Maybe just wait until the morning, she might have met some friends, left her phone somewhere, or run out of credit. I think, after everything that has happened today it has made us all jumpy and imagining the worst. Try and rest, then start again in the morning, if she hasn't turned up or contacted you. I need to go to bed now, I'm exhausted. Let me know tomorrow and we can take it from there. Now try not to worry.'

Aurelio gave a hesitant smile and nodded. 'Yes you're right, I do think the past events have freaked me out. I'll go back to the hostel and try and rest. She might have even come back,' he added hopefully, but with little conviction. After saying goodnight, he went down the steps and into the night. Susan went slowly up to her room and turned on the light. The bed looked so inviting, she could barely get undressed and into to her pyjamas quickly enough. There wasn't a hope of trying to read even a few pages of her book. Switching off the light, Susan flopped gratefully onto the bed. But sleep did not come as easily as she had thought it would. Lying there in the darkness, faces swirled around in her thoughts. Children floating facedown in the water, their dark hair fanning out around them like exotic pieces of seaweed. The poor, sad face of the African, dead in the street, and finally a parade of faces looming out from the pages of the mug shot files. How was she ever going to get to sleep with all that going on in her head? The night stretched on, would sleep ever come?

Chapter 6

Susan must have drifted off finally, for when she awoke, a brilliant sunlight filled the room, and she could hear the sound of people having breakfast on the terrace below. She lay there for a while playing back the events from last night in her mind. She felt a sadness combined with hope and anticipation that she would be spending more time with the commissario today. Susan also thought again of Aurelio's anxiety about Angela, she hoped that Angela had returned and all was well. She showered and dressed, choosing a comfortable outfit of cool cotton pants and a soft muslin top. Happy Birthday to me. How funny, she hadn't even had time to think about it.... Susan went down to have her breakfast. Although it was after nine, there were still a few guests enjoying a variety of coffees and a selection of freshly baked pastries set out on the long table at the side of the terrace. A bowl of fresh fruit stood at the end. She selected a golden peach and ordered a caffe latte from the waiter, before sitting down at a small table. She nodded to a few of the other guests she had seen around Villa Nettuno, and then began to check her phone for messages. There were two from her children checking to see how she was and wishing her a happy birthday, and a missed call from Commissario

Lombardo. I'll ring back after breakfast, Susan thought, it can't be that urgent.

She had just finished eating, when she saw the commissario coming through the reception area. She got up quickly and went out to meet him. 'I was just going to finish breakfast, and then call you back.'

'I've come about Angela, remember the girl on Isola Bella, the one who was with Aurelio, she's missing.... from last night. I wanted to ask if you had seen her, or if she'd contacted you at all?'

'No, sorry. Aurelio was here last night, asking the same thing. I haven't seen her since yesterday. After we left Isola Bella, we parted ways, and I haven't seen or heard from her since. What could have happened to her?'

'That's what we have to find out, I only knew she was missing this morning, Aurelio came to the Questura and told us, he was in a terrible state. Apparently he didn't get much sleep and had worked himself into a panic.'

'I know; he was pretty upset last night too. I told him to just wait until morning in case she had stayed with a friend and lost her phone, but it is a little disturbing, her just going off like that. She didn't seem the sort of person who'd just up and disappear without telling someone.'

'I hope her disappearance doesn't have any connection to her father, Rocco Salvino's business dealings, and Aurelio's family. Those standover men you identified yesterday are linked to the Saconnes, plus there's a dead African and last but definitely not least, a sea full of dead refugees, it's getting more and more crazy. I'm going to head over to Palermo now and see if the family's heard anything. I've asked Aurelio to stay here in Taormina in case she turns up. If you aren't busy today, would you mind meeting up with him and going over things, you never know one of you might remember something that could help. I think he also needs someone to keep an eye on him, otherwise he's likely to do something silly. He has a tendency to become over emotional, so a distraction would be good.'

'No, I haven't made any plans. I'll go round to the hostel now; I'll just get my bag.'

They walked down the steps together, then went their separate ways. Susan followed the tourist map she'd picked up from the reception desk and was happy to see that the hostel was easy to get to, down in an area near Isola Bella. She remembered Angela saying something about it on their way back from the island. Taking the funicular down to the car park/bus station and following the map around the road, Susan finally came to the youth hostel. Washing flapped from the windows and loud music was coming from somewhere inside. She opened the door and went in. There was a small reception desk with pigeon holes and hooks for room keys hanging behind it. Various pieces of luggage, mainly rucksacks were piled up in a corner. There was no one around. She rang the bell on the desk and then again, longer and louder, finally a little old man came out from behind a cutained door.

'Si,' he mumbled showing an almost toothless smile.

'Buongiorno,' Susan answered. 'I'm looking for Aurelio, is he here?'

The old man shook his head, 'no,' then pointed to the door leading to the street, 'gone......' 'I'll wait here until he gets back if that's alright,' Susan spoke slowly, pointing to an old battered armchair on which she proceeded to sit.

The old man didn't seem to mind and went back through the curtained door leaving Susan alone in the foyer. At least an hour had passed before Susan finally saw Aurelio coming through the door, his face flushed from the heat and his eyes full of frustration and worry.

'Ah! I still don't know where she has gone, no one seems to know, she's just vanished, I don't know where to look next.'

Susan looked at him equally puzzled, not knowing what to say or do, but wishing all the same, that she could give him some sort of comfort.

'The commissario is doing all he can to help,' Susan replied, hoping that would give him some sort of reassurance.

'I know, I know,' he said, looking totally exhausted. 'It is just so unlike her.'

'Let's just sit for a while and have a drink, maybe by sitting quietly and going back over things something might come back, running around like crazy won't do us any good. Something must happen sooner or later. She can't have just disappeared like that, too many people will miss her.' Susan tried to keep a calmness in her voice even though she didn't feel it.

'There are some very powerful people in her family, I'm sure they will get to the bottom of this,' Aurelio said thoughtfully, a touch of apprehension in his voice.

They walked slowly down the road towards a café, it's solitary umbrella making dancing patterns in the shade as it fluttered weakly in the heat.

'Let's sit down here and try and work out what has happened,' Susan said. A young girl came out ready to take their order. 'What will you have Aurelio, a beer?' 'Yes,' he answered wearily. 'Two beers,' Susan told the girl '…. you'd better make them large ones…'

It was so hot, the heat from the road rose through the air boosted by the traffic passing by. It was hard to imagine that across the road and a few steps down, was the beautiful cool water of the sea.

In less than no time the girl was back, bringing two large beers, beads of condensation already gathering on the sides of the bottles, as another gust of heat hit them. They gratefully raised the bottles to their mouths and swallowed the icy drink with relief.

They were just beginning to relax a little when Aurelio's phone started beeping, he grabbed it out of his pocket quickly and looked at the message... 'It's Angela's mother, she's been trying to get hold of her and can't, she's worried and wants to know if I know why she's not picking up her phone. God! What should I say..... that she's missing? I can't do that. I'll try and stall her, tell her she's gone on a hike with some university friends somewhere in the mountains, and she's probably out of signal range. Hopefully, that will stop her from worrying for a while, until we can sort it out.' He tapped out a message feverishly and then drained his beer. 'I've got to go, speak to a few people, some of her friends, maybe they saw her before, it's just not like her.' His face looked puzzled, his eyes reddened from lack of sleep.

'I'll come with you,' Susan said. 'I want to know as well. If I stay here by myself, I'll go crazy.' The commissario's words came back to her. 'Keep an eye on him, who knows what he might do.'

They set off slowly up the road towards the funicular, deep in thought. Both mulling over what they should do next, and where to go. They sat silently side by side waiting for the funicular ride to take them up to the center of the town. Not many people were around now, like most sensible people they were lying on the beach under striped umbrellas, swimming, or in the cool air-conditioned bars or trattorias, not tramping up and down the cobbled streets of Taormina. The ride brought them to the top of the town and as they were walking past the bus station, Aurelio suddenly stopped. 'What's he doing here?' He was looking over at a man who appeared to be gesturing threateningly as he spoke to a someone in the bus ticket booth. He was pointing angrily at his phone, then back to a person he was shouting at. They could only hear snatches of the conversation, but he was obviously not going anywhere until his questions had been answered.

Susan looked across, it was the short, fat man she had seen arguing with the African the night before. How could she forget a face like that, and furthermore, she had picked him out from a folder of mug shots at the Questura. 'I've seen that man before. Do you know him, Aurelio?' 'Yes, unfortunately I do, he's one of my uncle's lackeys. I wonder what he's up to?' Aurelio walked across towards the ticket box. 'Hey, Gian, what's up?'

'I'll be back in a minute,' he called back over his shoulder to Susan. 'Just wait there, I won't be long.'

At the sound of his name the man turned from the booth, and looked across at Aurelio. He was still gesturing angrily, his face dark with rage, his mouth twisted in an expression of simmering frustration. As Aurelio got closer, he flung a piece of paper at him. Aurelio quickly picked it up and led the man over to a far corner of the bus depot, well out of earshot. The sounds of blaring horns and bus drivers' assistants hanging off the sides and calling out the destinations, made hearing anything impossible anyway. The cacophony rose and fell as each bus arrived or departed. 'Catania, Catania, Savoca, Siracusa.' The depot was a major one, obvious by the wide ranging destinations screamed across the hot dusty earth... Red faced, harassed looking travellers looked around them in utter confusion, their limp clothes hanging from their sweaty bodies. Hats with the logos of popular brands or favourite tourist hot spots, squashed down on their heads. Whinging, exhausted children dragged along by family members, desperate to find their bus and get into the relative cool of the air conditioning inside. Susan looked around wishing she had just gone to the beach and left all this searching and carrying on to Aurelio and the Poliza de Stato, after all it wasn't her problem, she didn't even speak the language well enough to be of much help.

On the other side of the depot she could still see Aurelio and the other man deep in conversation. What's that all about? Susan wondered, not for the first time. In the midst of those thoughts she was suddenly brought back to earth by a voice at her ear. 'Sorry, I have to go to Palermo tonight, something has come up and my family needs me.' Aurelio's face seemed drawn and worried. Looking back over to where the two men had been talking, Susan saw that the other man was no longer there.

'What about Angela?' Susan asked. 'Surely you can't just leave now. Shouldn't we keep looking, she might be in trouble?'

'Oh, don't worry, I'm sure she'll turn up sooner or later,' Aurelio answered. 'She can look after herself, and the police are also looking. I bet she's just gone off on a spontaneous jaunt and will turn up tomorrow laughing at how we had taken this far too seriously.'

It all sounded a bit fake to Susan, only an hour ago he was desperate with worry, now he had made a complete turnaround. Well it was better she was out of it anyway, this was meant to be a holiday, and she was off to Cava D'Aliga in two days. I wonder if I'll hear from the commissario again? It would be nice to have some closure on that terrible refugee situation, Susan thought.

'Ok, I'll be off then. I hope all goes well, and you sort out your family problem. I'll give you my number. Maybe you could let me know if and when Angela turns up. I'm going back to Cava D'Aliga in a couple of days.'

'Will do.' Aurelio lent over and a gave her a quick peck on both cheeks. 'Thanks for being there and helping. I'll let you know if anything turns up.' He turned and went quickly out of the depot leaving Susan standing there in the middle of the chaos. How strange, she thought to herself, Aurelio's sudden change of behaviour, the almost desperate attempt to get away as fast as possible. It was weird, really weird. Oh well, that's it then. Susan made her way out of the craziness and down the street towards Villa Nettuno. As she walked, a car passed her, driving quickly down the road, a sleek, expensive grey limousine. Inside, she glimpsed Aurelio's face, he was talking animatedly to someone sitting back in the deep shadows of the car, and stranger still, behind the wheel was the fat, sweaty, man he had been talking to at the bus depot. That's odd. It's that Gianni, the face from the mug shot, his uncle's enforcer. Susan was thoughtful, puzzled by this new development. She continued along the footpath, wondering, not for the first time, what on earth was going on.

There were so many unanswered questions. Where was Angela? Why was Aurelio talking to Gianni? And the strangest one of all, why was Aurelio driving away with him? Hopefully it wouldn't be too long before her questions were answered.

Chapter 7

Palermo Central Station is such a strange, unsettling place, Commissario Lombardo thought as he watched the intense, and often anxious, expressions on peoples' faces as they hurried by. A loud argument between a harassed looking porter and an elderly woman near the baggage collection room echoing through the station's vast spaces, only confirming his opinion. The high ceilinged halls, which were large and airy, also helped magnify the clamorous sound of the many passengers. The sound of their hurrying footsteps, echoing, as they embarked on journeys to destinations which started and ended at this station.

Lombardo had just come from the bus terminal, after checking the arrivals from Catania and Modica. He was looking for a familiar face. He hadn't seen it yet, so he was now looking at train arrivals. He walked along leisurely, observing the throng of passengers, boarding and getting off the trains at this large terminal. It was the end of the line, unless you were taking an ongoing journey by bus, inland or further along the coast. Trapani, Terrasini, San Vito Lo Capo, Selinunte......Suddenly, amidst the throng of passengers moving through the station, the flash of a face, someone well known to him, caught his eye....
'Gino!' He called out to a balding, thin man who was making

his way quickly towards the entrance which led out onto the busy pavements and into the chaotic traffic. Friday afternoon was not the best time to be around here, he thought wearily. He had been on the road nonstop since leaving Taormina mid-morning. A filled panino and a bottle of water were all that he had managed to eat and drink, now it was close to three o'clock. 'Hey Gino!' He shouted again... now in hot pursuit of his fast-moving quarry... slightly breathless, he finally caught up with the man. Holding tightly to his arm in case he made a sudden run for it, Lombardo managed to gasp, 'Gino, didn't you hear me call out to you?' The man dropped his head muttering slowly.... 'Oh, was that you, Commissario, calling out? I didn't realise it was you.' His shifty eyes failed to make contact as he tried to wriggle free from the commissario's grasp.

'Just come over here for a minute,' Lombardo pulled him out of the way of the busy path of travellers, towards a slightly quieter section. Under one of the colonnaded verandahs, at the side of the building, he continued the conversation. 'Gino, I only wanted to ask you a couple of questions. I was wondering if you had seen either of the Scarsi brothers around, over the past few days?'

The Scarsi brothers were notorious thugs who worked as stand over men, keeping the ragtag groups of refugee workers under control. They organised the buses that took these poor men, and sometimes women as well, to farming locations high up in the desolate rocky hills. There, these poor people worked as slave labour, planting, harvesting, and loading trucks full of the fresh produce which was then transported to the super-markets and restaurants in Sicily and other parts of Southern Italy. The workers toiled under incredibly harsh conditions, often working off a debt for just having been picked up from refugee centres or secret boat landings, in out of the way inlets around the island. If they tried to escape they were beaten and sometimes maimed as an example to others who might have been thinking of doing the same thing. The conditions they were housed in were worse than many animal sheds and they were fed not much better.

Gino was a small-time, odd job man who worked for several families. He ran messages, sold pieces of information, and, he was also Lombardo's informant. Lombardo was looking for any information about new arrivals of refugees or any expected boats that were due along the coast.

'No, no,' Gino twisted and turned, trying to escape from Lombardo's grasp. 'I don't know anything, I haven't heard anything, I'd tell you if I had, truly Commissario.' Lombardo finally released him. 'Don't go too far away Gino, I'll want to speak to you again,' he called out to his quickly disappearing back, as he scurried away through the crowds. Leaving the terminus, Lormbardo turned, and looked back, catching a glimpse of the huge brooding relief of Mount Pellegrino. It was always there, a backdrop to the city, like a sentinel keeping watch over its inhabitants. There was a cave perched up there, close to the summit, which housed a shrine devoted to Saint Rosalia, the patron saint of Palermo. She was there to keep the city and her citizens safe. He always found comfort looking at that mountain, it had been a constant throughout his life even when things had been at their worst.

Lombardo continued out into the street, walking with a purpose towards Via Roma, navigating the busy traffic from the roundabout and crossing over between the crazily driven buses, cars, and motorbikes. After about five hundred metres, he turned into one of the narrow, shadowy, laneways which ran off the busy main road like a series of rabbit warrens. There, in that crowded, cramped area were many small shops, which often gave no indication of what their business was, nor, were there any obvious signs of customers. People from the neighbourhood, had, over time, pulled old rickety armchairs and battered tables on to the cobbled pathway, building a makeshift, communal living room where residents could gather in the cool of the evening. Leaving their cramped, overheated apartments, they socialised with neighbours and watched the world go by. Coming to a corner, he turned left and walked on further until he came to a small, dark building, it's one window and a battered brown metal door both open to let some air into the room. Looking inside, he saw a group of women and girls. Some were sitting in front of garish, cheap-looking mirrors, while others stood behind them doing their hair. Some were giving manicures or facials to the other customers in the salon. Several small children slept, wrapped in shawls, on a mattress in the corner, the heat and the soft murmur of voices lulling them into deep contented dreams.

As Lombardo put his head through the open window, the women stopped talking and looked at him. Their faces questioning, but showing no fear.

'Hi, Rose, could I have a quick word with you?' One of the women, who had been in the middle of plaiting a woman's hair into intricate braids, came over to him. She was tall, with an almost regal air about her. Her features were fine and quite beautiful. Dark eyes looked at Lombardo with a slightly apprehensive expression. A brightly patterned scarf was tied around her hair and her arms jangled with many brightly coloured bracelets. 'Si, Commissario,' she answered quietly, in lightly accented Italian. The other women in the room had stopped what they were doing and watched warily as Rose went over to the window. One of the babies on the mattress started to cry and a woman went over to it quickly, hushing gently, whilst patting it back to sleep.

'I was wondering where I could find Jonno?' Lombardo spoke quietly, but with an element of firmness. He had known Rose for a few years now. She had been rescued from a trafficking gang which specialised in the lucrative prostitution trade, mainly in the busy tourist towns of Sicily. She, along with others, had been found after a tip-off from one of Lombardo's informants, who had, for some reason, developed a conscience. His uncle, a priest, from a diocese in Monte san Pietro, near the Palermo Cathedral, had accompanied him, along with several other police officers. They had found fifteen girls and young women being held prisoner in a huge house in Santa Flavia. Many of them had been drugged and forced into a life of unbelievable cruelty and depravity. His uncle's parishioners had taken the women under their wings, teaching them skills and setting them up in small businesses, such as salons, cafes, and child care. The younger girls were put into school to finish their education and now some of them were well on the way to continuing their further studies in teaching, nursing, or law.

This was one of the businesses, a thriving beauty salon specialising in African beauty treatments and hairstyling.

Rose looked down at the floor, 'I, I haven't seen him for a few days, he said he was going to Catania, someone rang and said they had a job for him.'

'Do you know who rang, and what sort of job it was?' Lombardo looked skeptical... 'No, it was someone Doni knew, that's all I know....'

Doni was another young man, who, like Jonno, was looking to fit in, be part of a gang. Wanting the good things in life without worrying too much about what the payment for those good things was likely to be. The good things in life always came with a high price, maybe not straight away but it would come... This was not good news.

Lombardo sighed... this was such a long, frustrating process. Of course these women were not forthcoming, they were extremely wary of the law, and with what they had been through, who could blame them.

All of them had made the long journey from within Africa. Although the actual countries may have been different and the way they had got here, their reasons for taking that difficult, and often dangerous journey were the same. An escape from poverty, abuse, and the chance of a better life. Their experiences were not that different either. Vulnerable, abused, exploited, the shocking things these women had been through were often unimaginable. What people were capable of made Lombardo despair...

It was a familiar story, not just here, but throughout Europe and beyond. Women rescued, then taken in and helped by charity groups working in and around Palermo, including one which was run by Lombardo's uncle.

Lombardo and the Poliza di Stato had, on numerous occasions, been called to extract women and children from dangerous circumstances. Situations that had sometimes needed firepower combined with the full force of the law, to rescue them. After that, they needed to be housed, taught skills which enabled them to become independent, and their children put into schools. They also had to feel safe, and that was often the hardest thing of all. There were usually no consistent men in their lives. A common thread through these pitiful histories was that they had been exploited and then deserted by men. Fathers, brothers, husbands, uncles. Their intentions may have started as well-meaning, but along the way these men also fell victim to exploitation and violence, victims of cruel labour gangs, or the smuggling trade, which often resulted in death. The more enterprising had run off or allied themselves with gangs for protection, but which had ended up exploiting them even further.

It was very hard to keep yourself out of the hands of the various families who waited to snap up these poor people when they were at their most vulnerable.

Jonno, was Rose's brother, an unfortunate 'chancer' not too bright and always just one step ahead of the police, until he tripped up, which happened quite often. He wasn't usually violent, although he did have a quick temper. Circumstances and what life had dished up to him, had made him the person he was today. He was known more as an energetic petty criminal, easily manipulated by those who were cleverer.... always in with a chance. Acting first and thinking later was his style.

Lombardo also knew, that considering the circles Jonno moved in, he was likely to have heard about any new schemes being hatched that involved people smugglers, and any businesses in the area that suddenly needed extra cheap labour. It was just a matter of tracking him down, then maybe, after being given a name or two, identify who could had given the order for the bloodbath in the waters around Isola Bella and the reasons behind it.

'If he gets in touch let him know I'd like a word with him. I'll be here for a couple of days.' Rose slowly nodded and turned back to her client. The room remained silent as he left.

Lombardo continued down the alleyway until he finally came back onto Via Roma. He was getting hotter and more tired and regretted not taking the car, but it was too late to turn back now, and he still wanted to call in at his uncle's place and find out if he had heard anything about the mass murders on Isola Bella. He wasn't far from headquarters, but he thought he would give that a miss. He didn't want to draw any attention to himself from the people there, not until it was absolutely necessary and there was no other choice. Much better not to stir the hornet's nest until he had exhausted all options, so he kept on walking.

Chapter 8

Susan slowly climbed the seemingly endless steps up to Villa Nettuno. She was still thinking about the events that had taken place earlier at the bus terminus and then afterwards, witnessing Aurelio being suddenly driven away by a man with known criminal connections.

So many unanswered questions. What had Aurelio been talking to that man about and why had his behaviour changed so quickly after the meeting? Not to mention the mysterious person he was deep in conversation with, in the back seat of the car.

It was all so confusing. Susan suddenly felt an overwhelming sense of loneliness. So far from home and family. She walked into the reception area, thank goodness Salvo wasn't on the desk and she could just take the key without having to indulge in light chatter. She opened the door, threw her bag down, and flopped on the bed. As she lay there, finally relaxing, she noticed a piece of paper stuck under the bedside lamp. What was that she thought, a funicular ticket or a receipt for something? Stretching out she pulled it from beneath the lamp base. It was a page torn from a note pad, with the University of Palermo letterhead at the top. A message had been written in hastily scribbled pencil.

'Susan, I have had to leave Taormina suddenly, sorry for not saying goodbye, but I believe something is not right with Aurelio. I saw a message that came through on his phone when he was out. I thought it might have been urgent so I read it. It was from his cousin, who is a very bad person, telling him about an important family meeting in Santa Flavia tomorrow night that he must attend. I no longer feel safe in his company so I'm going to stay with some relatives in Savoca for a while. Please don't worry about me, I hope we can meet again. Angela.'

How strange, but at least things were a little clearer and she now knew that Angela was alright. The events over the last couple of days had made Susan more curious, and she also felt a responsibility to get to the bottom of that awful massacre. The feelings of tiredness and loneliness had disappeared. A plan was now forming in Susan's mind. I think it's time for me to leave Taormina, there's no reason to stay anymore. I'll go back to Cava D'Aliga tomorrow, drop off my things, and then go on to Palermo and talk to the commissario about Angela's note, it might be helpful. I have a strong feeling that everything that happened earlier leads back to Palermo. I could also see Lucie while I am there. I did promise her I would try, and this seems like the perfect opportunity.

Lucie di Romano was a friend Susan had made a few years ago on an earlier trip to Palermo. She had been staying in Santa Flavia and often went to Palermo on the train to visit the cathedral, eat lunch at one of her favourite trattorias in the Vuccira, and then call into a special ceramic shop to buy a few brightly painted tiles to add to her collection at home. One afternoon, on the way back to Santa Flavia, she had sat next to a woman on the train who had struck up a conversation with her. Lucie had been starved for a chat with someone from outside Italy. She was American, but of Italian heritage, and had come back to Italy, specifically Palermo, as a young woman. She had then married and had four daughters. Her husband was connected to a family, but there had been a falling out over a business deal. He suddenly had to leave and go into exile in Malta. If she wanted to see him, Lucie had to go there. It was not safe for him to come back, and, according to her, it would be a very long time before he could. She was left to raise her daughters alone with the often unwanted help from interfering and critical family members, mainly her mother-in-law and sister-in-law, both of whom held traditional and antiquated ideas on how a woman should behave. Because she had come from outside, she would never be able to run a house or raise children properly. Years of mental abuse from these women had chipped away at her belief in herself and overall happiness. Both of them had finally become too old to bother her anymore, moving to Monreale to stay with an older brother and his family, much to Lucie's relief.

Lucie lived in an apartment in Bagheria, not far from where Susan was staying. They had got on so well, that they arranged to meet up for dinner later that evening. Over dinner, in a restaurant overlooking the habour of Porticello, Lucie continued with her story. She had got a job as a chef in a five-star hotel in Palermo and still worked there. She commuted from Bagheria each day. Now there was only one daughter still at home, and she was in her final year of high school.

She was a lonely woman, who had found it difficult to keep living in Sicily after her husband left, especially with the relentless interference from his mother and sister, but, there seemed nowhere else she could go. Over the years, the difficult circumstances she had found herself in had given her self-confidence a beating, and also her health. She was now a diabetic, but did little to take care of herself. Overworked and depressed, her parents both dead and estranged from her siblings, returning to America was not an option as far as she was concerned. She seemed resigned to spending the rest of her days in Bagheria. Even though she was the same age as Susan, she had lost the will to travel or do things that might help her feel better about the position she had found herself in. It was as if all the fight had gone out of her. Susan was astonished to learn that her second daughter was married to someone in the Carabinieri stationed in Naples, but Lucie had never been there for a visit. Naples wasn't that far away, just a train ride. Susan had felt sorry for her and made an even greater effort to stay in touch.

I guess I'd better let them know downstairs that I'll be leaving a day early Susan thought. Knowing how interested they would be in why she had decided to leave a day earlier, she decided to tell them that she had had an unexpected invitation to go and stay with a friend in Palermo. That was true and should keep them happy.

The next morning after a surprisingly deep and untroubled sleep, she was packed and ready to catch the ten am. train from Giardini Naxos. Salvo had rung a taxi and after settling the bill she said goodbye, promising to come back soon.

Susan loved Giardini Naxos railway station. Inaugurated in 1866, it was kept in the most beautiful condition. Tiled platforms, iron awnings, beautiful shrubs and plants in decorated pots, and a glimpse of the blue, blue sea beyond, with yachts and small cruisers bobbing on the waves. There was also a bustling, friendly coffee shop. The smell of coffee and warm cornettoes wafted out of its doorway. Susan hadn't felt like breakfast before she left the hotel and had just had a quick espresso for an energy boost. Now after buying her ticket, a train to Syracuse, change, and another train to Sampieri, finishing with a short taxi ride to Cava D'Aliga, she felt like a frothy cappuccino and a brioche or cornetto. She went inside the cafeteria and stood up at the counter. 'A cappuccino and a ......' she pointed to one of the still warm, lightly sugar-dusted pastries under the cover of the counter. When the hot coffee was put down in front of her Susan took the pastry and coffee and went and sat at a small table where she could still see the platform and train schedule outside. Her train was due in about twenty minutes, there was still plenty of time.

The train came on time and Susan was able to sit next to the window. She settled gratefully into the comfortable seat and gazed outside at the already busy water. Motor boats roared up and down and pleasure cruisers were setting off for the day, visiting some of the small islands nearby. There was a sharp whistle and off the train went. The journey should take about two hours, then a wait of about forty-five minutes at Syracuse, and after another hour and fifteen minutes she would arrive in Sampieri.

Susan looked across at her travelling companions, a woman talking non-stop on her phone, a man with his head deep in a newspaper and opposite her a nun in a grey habit, eating something out of a plastic container. She didn't look Italian but rather more Asian, possibly Filipina. Susan smiled across at her and she smiled back. 'Buongiorno.' 'Buongiorno,' the nun replied. 'Do you speak English?' She added.

'Yes,' Susan replied, surprised at hearing the nun addressing her in clear English. 'Where are you from?' Susan continued...

Originally from Cambodia, but I have been in Rome for a short break and now I am on my way back to Syracuse where I work with refugees. My name is Sister Annuncia.'

'So nice to meet you, I'm Susan and I'm from Australia. I'm here on a holiday.'

They settled into an easy conversation as the train wound its way through the coastal villages and larger towns of eastern Sicily. Sister Annuncia had many stories to tell, describing the poor souls who ended up in the refuge she and the other sisters ran. People who had been fished out of the sea and deposited on their doorstep by the authorities who didn't know what else to do with them. Wearing only the clothes on their backs, these men, women, and children were traumatised, hungry, and had lost all hope. She and her fellow sisters tried to make things a little better. Kind words, hot food, and a safe place to stay. The new arrivals were taught Italian, and the skills needed to help them fit into their new home and become independent. The men were found paying jobs in the markets and businesses around the habour and other places in and around Syracuse. The women were often employed in restaurants, in child care, or in the markets. The locals were pleased to help, as many of them had come from impoverished backgrounds themselves and understood only too well the need to be compassionate, but also offer practical help as well. As Susan listened to the nun's stories, fascinated by how resilient those people were, her mind went back to the broken bodies in the water off Isola Bella. The nun's kind voice and non-judgmental attitude made Susan relax and feel comfortable talking to her. Suddenly, she found herself recounting the events from three days ago to the kind-faced nun sitting opposite her on a train speeding through the wild, rocky Sicilian landscape. Once those first tentative words left her mouth, the shock, sadness, and anger all came out in a torrent of words. Sister Annuncia sat in silence as Susan talked on. 'There were little children, their broken bodies hidden under their mothers', young men full of hope for the future, old people clinging to each other......'Susan went on. 'The violence I saw in that boat and in the water around it, was shocking. How could people do that to others? They hadn't done anything; they were vulnerable.... sitting ducks, caught in the middle of a vendetta or grievance. My heart breaks every time I think of that scene. Have you ever heard of something like that happening before, Sister?' Susan sat back against her seat, emotionally exhausted after reaching the end of that unexpected outpouring. 'Have you ever seen such violence inflicted on defenseless people...?'

The nun sat silently, she didn't speak for a few minutes. Finally, in a quiet voice, she answered. 'My family lived through the time of Pol Pot.' She looked across at Susan as if waiting for a reaction. Susan sat still, wondering how she should respond. What could you say...of course, how thoughtless of me not to realise that. How old would she have been? Sister Annuncia looked as if she was in her thirties, it was hard to tell with nuns, their clear, bright, gentle faces often belied their real age. Pol Pot's regime lasted from nineteen seventy- five until nineteen seventy-nine, so, if she was in her early forties now she would have been a very small child.

The silence in the carriage continued to hang between them as the Sicilian landscape swept by outside the windows. Dry, brown craggy mountains on one side and a clear blue sea, punctuated with small seaside communities full of holidaymakers on the other. Where was God, and why did he allow these awful things to happen? Surely it would test one's faith, Susan couldn't help but think...

'What did you think of Rome?' Susan finally spoke. Sister Annuncia answered straight away glad of the chance to break the silence. 'I found it rather exciting, meeting different nuns from other parts of the world and being in such a busy city, but I am also glad to be going back to my work in Syracuse. Yes, there is certainly a lot to see and do there.' She reflected, smiling at Susan.

The train was now passing through the outskirts of Syracuse. Hastily built, ragged, brown and grey apartment blocks were strategically placed in between sprawling factories. Rows of washing hung from the cramped balconies. Occasionally, the sight of bright flowers in planters on those same balconies, showed an attempt by a resident to brighten their drab home. Dry, long, yellow grass grew on the sides of the railway tracks.

Why did the edge of towns and cities always look so sad and unwelcoming? Susan couldn't help thinking. As the train moved on things started to look a little better and after another ten minutes of stopping and starting, they finally arrived. Sister Annuncia took her small suitcase down from the overhead luggage rack, while Susan went towards the luggage storage shelves near the door. 'It was lovely to meet you,' Susan said, giving the nun a warm hug and kissing her on both cheeks, Sister Annuncia responded with equal warmness. 'Here is my email and phone number,' Susan handed her a card,

'Here is my address and number too,' the nun hastily writing them down on a piece of paper.

'I'd really like to visit your refugee centre some time,' Susan said, as she took the paper. After they stepped down from the train, they hugged again and promised to stay in touch. The nun walked quickly towards the station exit and Susan went to look at the departure board to check the time of her onward journey to Sampieri.

The station was extremely quiet. It reminded Susan of the railway stations you sometimes saw in movies set in the wild west. Long deserted platforms stretched ahead ending in a desolate, dry, flat, no man's land. It wouldn't have surprised Susan to see a gunslinger suddenly appear at the end of a platform with his gun out, ready to shoot. Looking up at the departures board, she saw that her train was due to leave in thirty minutes from platform two B. Where on earth was two B? She scanned the platform numbers but could only see two. It was another platform across, so she went down the stairs, through the passage, and up on to the other side. She put her case down and sat. No one else was on the platform and as she looked around Susan could only see a few other people waiting on the other side. The weather was very hot, thank goodness there is still enough water in my bottle, she thought. After she had been sitting for about ten minutes, a man suddenly appeared, he was wearing the uniform of a station employee. 'Where are you going?' He asked. 'Sampieri.....Oh, you need to go to platform two B.'

'Where on earth is that?' Susan responded in an exasperated voice. 'Follow me, I'll show you.'

Back they went, down the stairs and on to the original platform, then over to a far corner. Two B said a small sign. 'Grazie,' said Susan gratefully. How weird is that odd platform number. At least the man had thought to let her know and not leave her sitting there. There is kindness and also a willingness to help, which made her love Sicilians even more.

After waiting for twenty more minutes the train rolled into the station, a small local train with rattily open windows. Susan climbed up, dragging the suitcase behind her, and found a seat where she could put the case out of the way of other travellers. There was a long whistle and off the train went. There weren't many people on the train, a group of German backpackers and a couple of women laden with bags, obviously coming home from the market. Sitting back in her seat Susan stared out the window and relaxed, in just over an hour she would arrive in Sampieri. I'd better message Anna to pick me up from the station, she thought, as she got out her phone.

There were three missed calls and two messages, damn, the phone had been on silent. They were all from a number she didn't recognise.

Chapter 9

Capo was the area Lombardo had grown up in, a mixture of decay and splendor. A densely packed neighbourhood full of narrow alleyways where children played and deals were done. Walking over from Via Roma to Via Maqueda and down a narrow street into Piazza Sant Onofrio, he felt his body relax after the chaos of the station. He then made a beeline towards the Bar Nevada. A cool drink and a bit of a chat were what he wanted before he went on to his uncle's place. The bar was full of noisy regulars enjoying a late afternoon get together. Virginia and Pino were at their usual places, Pino behind the bar and Virginia at her table out front. They had both grown up with Lombardo, attending the local school, playing in the alleyways, smoking their first cigarette together, before going their separate ways. Lombardo going on to university followed by five years of further study in London, and Virginia and Pino falling in love and making their own life, staying in Capo. They greeted him cheerfully, pulling up a chair at the table and placing a large icy beer in front of him.

'Luca, you look exhausted, what on earth have you been doing?

Have you been walking?' The questions came thick and fast.

Lombardo laughed… 'Just let me drink, Gina, and then I'll talk.'

She sat back and looked at him with concern. 'Caro, Luca, I'm just a bit excited to see you, it's been a while, you know.' Virginia (Gina) was one of the calmest, and kindest people he knew. She was a mountain of a woman, a huge smiling buddha. Sitting out the front of Bar Nevada every day, Gina held court like a benevolent queen. She was many things to many people in the neighbourhood. A mother figure, offering a comforting shoulder to lean on, a psychologist, a dispenser of welfare, a marriage guidance counsellor, and a childminder in an emergency. Finally, Lombardo felt refreshed enough to answer the questions being flung at him. 'It's ok, I walked from the station. I should have taken the car but when I realised it was too late. I also didn't want to be bothered with finding parking as well. I just didn't realise how hot it was. I had to pay a visit to some people along the way too.'

'What are you doing here though? I thought you were working in Taormina, bit too upmarket for you, is it? Needed to come back to the neighborhood, I can understand that,' one of the regulars spoke up from a table on the far side of the bar. It was almost hanging over the footpath. Bar Nevada's haphazard seating arrangements were well known and it was not unheard of for customers to bring chairs from their nearby houses if they had run out of things to sit on. 'Yes, very true,' Lombardo laughed. 'Now, tell me what's been happening around here, any news? What I have missed?'

Several voices spoke at once, the birth of a grandchild, a few romances, a young boy who had ridden a motorbike crazily down by the docks and ended up in a hospital with two broken legs, and a dodgy affair between one of the Eastern European workers that helped in the Vucciria, and the wife of Georgio, a chef on a cruise ship, who only came home twice a year. Their barely concealed feelings for each other had kept the neighbourhood enthralled. 'It was better than the daily soap operas,' someone piped up.

'Then there was the fight last week...' Pino joined in, but in a more subdued voice. Lombardo looked across at him. He was polishing some glasses behind the counter, a plate of freshly filled paninis in front of him. 'A gang of those asylum seekers from the refuge centre in Albergheria were down near Quattro Canti last weekend, don't know what they were up to, some said they were trying to force some of the migrants in the souvenir businesses to pay for protection. Don't those people already pay the Saconne family... can't those poor buggers get a break?'

'What happened then?' Lombardo asked, his interest piqued. The man in the far corner took up the story.

'Well, that other gang, mainly young locals from around here and a bit further down, didn't like it. I think they might have been egged on by the Saconnes' wanting to stir up trouble, as well as sending a warning to others who might also be thinking of trying to edge in on their business. There's a lot of competition now, it's a bit crazy if you ask me. Anyway,' he continued, 'there was an almighty fight out there, it frightened some of the horses and they ran off down the road, luckily there were no passengers in the carriages at the time. The guys in charge of the horses were furious, it was a bloody nightmare, to make matters worse the local boys had got hold of a gun and there were quite a few knives as well. Two of the refugees died, one shot in the neck and another stabbed. A couple from the other side had a few nasty stab wounds, but survived. It gave everyone a real shock I can tell you. We knew there were tensions but no idea things were that bad.'

The other customers nodded their heads in agreement, Pino adding, 'I don't know how they are going to fix this? Your uncle, Father Benedict, is trying to work something out between them, but when you've got two groups of hotheaded youngsters it's hard to find a middle ground. I can't help but be suspicious about who is really behind it, stirring things up and bringing trouble back to the neighbourhood. I thought that was all behind us, it appears I was wrong.' Everyone was quiet, deep in their own thoughts. This area had certainly had its fair share of tensions and blood feuds which had been played out in its streets, but over the last few years' things had settled down and people relaxed more. Now it seemed that something or someone was stirring the pot. Instead of ancient family disputes, regular flare-ups caused by racial tensions were more the norm. New arrivals without any proper social networks and unfamiliar with their new country were met with suspicion and sometimes animosity by the local people. The fear of job losses and an extra strain on already overburdened social services networks made things extremely volatile.

'Ready for another?' Pino called out to Lombardo. 'No thanks, I'd better be off, got to call in and see what my uncle has been up to. Keep well all of you, great to catch up.' They said their goodbyes, and Lombardo started walking further on down the narrow street. It was now filled with people coming home from work. He pressed hard against the walls of houses, keeping right away from the edge of the footpath, as bikes hurtled down the uneven, cobbled laneway. Turning off into a noisy side street, he had to duck and weave to avoid a soccer ball coming his way. Deftly, he moved his foot and sent the ball back to the kicker, a young boy with the biggest grin he had ever seen. Father Benedict was sitting out the front of a building that looked like it had once been a factory of some kind. The doors and windows were wide open and from inside came the voices of children reciting what sounded like poetry. Outside, others were engaged in a vigorous game of football. When Father Benedict saw Lombardo, he got up from the stool he had been sitting on and came towards him smiling. 'Luca, it's so good to see you,' and gave him an affectionate hug. Lombardo returned the embrace.

'I was in the area and thought I'd call in. I can't let an opportunity go by without catching up with my favourite uncle. How are things?' he continued.

'Not bad, not bad,' his uncle answered, nodding.

Father Benedict was a man of medium height with an almost completely bald head. He had the bluest, most sparkly eyes which were framed by scores of laugh lines, and the warmest smile. It was a smile that could calm the most traumatised child, something which he had had to do many times. He was dressed in a faded pair of blue jeans and a pink and black shirt which bore the logo of his favourite football team, Palermo. Father Benedict had run this children's club out of the disused factory for over ten years. The centre had been gifted the building by the owner in gratitude for what he did for the young people in the area. Children played a sport, new arrivals had language lessons, there was a mini gymnasium, a small kitchen and in one corner some bunk beds. Sometimes, for a variety of reasons, children could find themselves with nowhere to sleep, they knew that Father Benedict's house was always open. You could get something to eat, somewhere to sleep, and someone who would always listen. Although Lombardo was a regular visitor, because of his work in Taormina, it had been a while since he had last been here. 'Come, we are just about to eat,' the priest said. The children who had been outside, stopped their game and followed the two men inside, jostling and laughing happily. The others, who had been studying, stopped and joined them. They first washed their hands and then sat down at a long trestle table. Father Benedict sat at one end with Lombardo beside him. Already placed on the table were overflowing bowls of pasta, plates of crusty bread, and other bowls of vegetables and fruit. Two women in the tiny kitchen were finishing up the washing of chopping boards and pots and pans. They were both African in appearance, possibly Nigerian. After they had finished, they joined the children at the table. As well as the local children, whose families had lived here for generations, there were also the newcomers, who now thought of themselves as locals too. Before everyone started filling the bowls in front of them, Father Benedict said a short grace, the children sat still in their seats barely able to keep their hunger at bay. When the prayer came to an end, all murmured a hurried, soft, 'amen.' Immediately the room was filled with the sound of children's happy voices. Bigger ones helped the smaller ones with the food, before eating themselves. There was such a strong sense of community within that room, and as Lombardo helped himself to the pasta con le sarde, he felt he was home. The meal passed, with lots of noisy conversation, about their day at school, what friends had been doing and their plans for the upcoming weekend.

After the table had been cleared away, and the dishes washed, the children settled down in front of a large, battered, old television, ready to watch a popular program, a well- known singing competition. They all had their favourite contestants and there was a lot of friendly rivalry.

While everyone was focused on the TV, Lombardo took the opportunity to have a private word with his uncle, out of earshot of the others.

'Have you seen Jonno lately? I called in and saw his sister on my way here. She said she hadn't seen him for a few days. He wasn't involved in that fracas the other night, was he?'

'Aaah, Jonno!' The priest sighed, and shook his head. Jonno had been a new arrival ten years ago. A traumatised boy, who had started on a journey from a faraway country with a family, and was now left with only one family member, a sister. Along the way, relatives had been lost to death, or the grabbing of opportunities which would only come once, and had to be taken up straight away. He had spent a lot of time with Father Benedict at the centre and had finished his schooling. Jonno had an almost feverish energy that could only be calmed after a game of football. He had started an apprenticeship with a carpenter and was doing well, but the lure of easy money and a dare-devil streak made him a target for the gangs that preyed on young men like him. He had a quick temper and took offence easily, it was hard to imagine that he would stay out of trouble, and he hadn't. He had had quite a few run-ins with the police, but so far avoided jail.

'That boy! I haven't heard if he was involved the other night, but I don't think so, it would certainly surprise me if he was. He is involved with some pretty dodgy people connected to the Saconnes and I've tried to warn him several times, but he just laughs it off and says they are looking after him, that I shouldn't worry, and all is good. The word on the street is that he has been given a spot to manage in the Mercato di Ballaro` and it's gone to his head a bit. I don't think he would be involved in a street brawl. He has moved up in the gang and been given more responsibilities, but my heart is heavy, as nothing good ever comes from being involved with the Saconnes.'

Lombardo's ears pricked up, the Saconnes again, they were part of Aurelio's family, his uncle, was the don. That was certainly worth following up, there was no such thing as a coincidence he thought.

As they sat in companionable silence, grateful for this rare time together, Lombardo's phone suddenly rang loudly, an unwelcome intrusion. He had turned it on silent while he was having dinner, who knows what he had missed. He walked outside, the phone to his ear. 'Pronto.'

'Good evening sir, it's me, Gianluca, I'm ringing from the Questura in Taormina. I've just had a call from Palermo, they've been trying to get hold of you. They didn't know where you were, and you haven't let anyone know your movements. There's a body down at the docks, and they think you might be interested.' 'Ok, thanks Gianluca, sorry, my mind's been on other things. I'm on my way. I'll let them know I'm coming.'

'I'll drive you,' Father Benedict said, as Lombardo briefly filled him in. Calling out his goodbyes to the children, he promised to call in again soon. As they hurried down to where his old fiat was parked, neither of them dared think whose body it might be.

Chapter 10

As the train finally pulled into Sampieri, it was with a sense of relief that Susan saw Anna standing by the car waiting for her, ready to drive her on to Cava D'Aliga. The last hour had been extremely stressful, to say the least. The missed phone calls and messages had been from Angela's aunt, whom she had been staying with in Savoca. She had been beside herself with worry and it had taken Susan a few minutes to understand what had happened. Finally, she had worked it out.

It seemed that earlier that day Angela had gone for a walk, saying she would only be gone for an hour or two, it was now five hours since they had last seen her. She hadn't taken her phone and they had found Susan's number and noted it was one of the last she had used. They had tried some other friends including Aurelio, but there had been no reply. They were out of their minds with worry especially after what had happened in Taormina. She had tried to calm the auntie, although she didn't feel calm herself. Finally passing on Commissario Lombardo's number, she reassured her that he was someone they could trust and she was sure he would help or know someone who could.

Getting down from the train, Susan walked quickly towards Anna and her car, grateful to see a happy face. They embraced, then Anna put the case in the boot. Anna and Susan had met a few years ago when Susan had found herself in Scicli, dragging a heavy suitcase along the bumpy cobbled streets and no taxi in sight. Hot, stressed and thirsty, a kind, elderly local, sitting in a shady piazza, directed her to Anna's family business. A travel agency, combined with a taxi service. Anna had rescued her and now, during Susan's regular visits to the area over the years, was there to drive her.

'How was Taormina?' Anna asked, looking at Susan sitting quietly beside her.

'I really don't know where to begin,' Susan sighed. 'It was a bit of a nightmare to be honest,' and Susan proceeded to give Anna an abridged version of the events over the past few days. It was difficult trying to put into a few sentences what had happened during the long anticipated few days in the luxurious hilly retreat. 'Well that's it, I think.' Anna's mouth was slightly open in shock and amazement. 'How awful, you poor thing, what a nightmare, so dreadful, well several dreadful things really. Finding the refugees, then seeing that African stabbed, as well as all those other strange goings on.' 'Yes,' Susan replied, tears came to her eyes as she thought back to the people in the boat. Would those terrible images ever leave her?

The drive along the road to Cava D'Aliga was calming. The clumps of prickly pear and out -of -control bougainvillea bushes on the side of the road, plus the golden light from the glorious Sicilian summer sun shining on the deep blue water, finally relaxed her. As several small stone cottages dotted about the dry dusty scrub appeared, she knew she was close to home. They drew up outside a narrow, double storied building painted a pale yellow. Opposite was a low wall with a metal chain running above it, and down further the yellow sand and small waves gently lapping the shore. Susan stood for a moment breathing in the salty air and letting the strengthening evening breeze ruffle her hair and skin.

Anna put the case down beside her. 'I'll leave you now.'

'Yes, yes, thank you so much, Anna. Would you mind taking me to the bus stop tomorrow morning? I've told my friend, who lives in Bagheria, I would spend a few days with her. I also wanted to speak to Commissario Lombardo about Angela going missing, that's if he is still in Palermo.'

'Sure, what time? There is a bus that goes at eleven am. if I remember from last time.'

'That's great. Thanks so much Anna. I'll see you then.'

'You should try and relax now,' Anna said, as she got into her car. 'Take a walk or a swim....'

'Will do...' Susan waved, then turned and opened the front door. It was cool inside, thanks to the curtains that had kept out most of the strong afternoon sun.

After a long drink of water, Susan sat down on the couch and looked at her phone. A message from Lucie, popped up asking what time her bus got in tomorrow, and where they would meet. Susan thought it would be easier to go to the hotel where she worked and messaged back the time. She'd better message the commissario while she was at it, so she sent a quick message letting him know her plans.

Now that was out of the way, she changed into her swim suit, put a sun dress over the top and headed out the door again. The road wasn't particularly busy, it was that in- between time when people had finished their beach day and were home preparing for their evening activities. Dinner, followed by an evening stroll, *una passeggiata,* was the usual ritual.

Susan hastily pulled off her sun dress and threw it onto the sand, then walked quickly into the sea. After paddling out a little way, she plunged into the waves feeling the coolness cover her body, and finally she relaxed. Lying on her back for several minutes, the earlier stress left her. Turning over slowly she moved through the water with strong strokes.

Susan must have stayed in the water longer than she had realised, the evening darkness was beginning to cover the sea and the wind had turned chilly. Reluctantly she swam back to shore.

Once inside the house she checked her phone. There was a message from the commissario. He was looking forward to their meeting tomorrow and for her to message him when she arrived in Palermo. After a quick shower, Susan once again left the house. She was tired but knew she had to eat. A dish of melanzane followed by pasta with zucchini and ricotta, and two glasses of a dry white wine made her even more desperate for sleep, so as soon as she had finished she paid the bill and went straight home, cleaned her teeth and fell straight into bed.

She awoke to the sounds of morning, people passing by the window on morning walks, the garbage collection truck thumping and rattling bins and the delivery vans making their drop offs of freshly baked bread and pastries to the cafes nearby.

Susan looked at her phone it was nearly eight, she had slept deeply without any dreams, thank goodness. After a shower, she walked down to the café on the corner to have a latte and pastry before she got ready for the journey to Palermo. She felt energised, and when she heard Anna's beep she was ready for what would be another long, long day.

After dropping her at the bus station, Susan said she would let Anna know when she would be back, and after a hug, said goodbye. The bus was already there, so after stowing her case underneath in the luggage storage, she climbed aboard and bought her ticket. The bus was about half full and Susan was able to sit by herself. After about fifteen minutes the bus set off. There were quite a few stops and the bus soon filled up. An elderly woman with a walking stick and several large bags sat down beside her and fell instantly asleep, her stick banging against Susan's leg. Being as unobtrusive as she could she moved it further back towards the woman, where it teetered precariously against one of her bags, Susan prayed that it wouldn't fall into the aisle and trip someone up. The bus moved up and around the mountainous road, leaving the coast and travelling inland. It made fewer stops and seemed to be on a steady path to its destination. The scenery consisted of farm land dotted with houses. Susan amused herself by comparing the different houses. Some, were at the end of long, tree lined avenues, which reminded her of one of her favourite movies Il Gattopardo, The Leopard. Huge houses with neglected terraces and fading white and green shutters, stood in what was once regal splendor, in the middle of nowhere. Their dry, sunburnt surroundings provided a stark backdrop to their crumbling former glory. Susan sat mesmerised, her face near the window. Then there were smaller houses that seemed more like animal stables. Sheep grazed in the fields, and in others, huge orchards stood waiting for next month's harvest season. Before she knew it the bus was pulling into a road stop. Some people got down, the elderly woman kept sleeping, and Susan tried to gently climb over the bags without waking her. She stirred slightly, but that was all. The café was crowded, people ordering an espresso or water and a snack. Taking an already filled panino, some water and ordering a coffee, Susan paid and then waited in the coffee line with her receipt.

Suddenly, there was a huge commotion from inside the bus, people craned their necks trying to look out the window to see what was happening. Two men, dragging a third, came down the steps of the bus, the one being dragged was struggling, calling out for help and crying loudly. 'It wasn't me, it wasn't me,' he screamed, trying to break free. One of the men hit him hard on the side of his head and he slumped down. They pulled him into a dark blue car parked at the side of the road stop. No one tried to stop them, everyone just stood and looked. Susan noticed two things, rather belatedly, she thought later, when she was describing the scene to Commissario Lombardo. One, that the man being grabbed was of African appearance, and two, that one of the men taking part in his abduction looked very familiar, exactly like the man at the bus station who had been talking to Aurelio and whom she had also seem before in the restaurant in Taormina. She would not forget that face easily, Gianni the enforcer.

She drank her coffee quickly and joined the other passengers reboarding the bus. People were mainly quiet, although a few spoke to each other in hushed whispers. The elderly woman was now awake and looked shocked by what had just happened. She sat muttering a litany of prayers and crossing herself. Susan gave her an apologetic smile as she tried to climb over her without causing too much trouble. After she'd sat down again and put the bags and walking stick back close to the woman, the driver checked the bus and they resumed their journey, minus one. Who was that one, and why had he been taken off the bus with such force? Had he been travelling alone, and if so, what would happen to his bag, if he had one. And on top of that, why was that creepy man there? He seemed to be everywhere. Susan puzzled over these questions for the rest of the journey. The other passengers either dozed or stared out of the window. It was as if nothing had happened.

The bus was now heading down towards the coast, the small beach towns passed by in a flash, Termini Imerese, Santa Flavia and on they went, finally pulling into the bus terminus behind the Palermo railway station.

After helping the elderly woman with her bags, Susan picked up her case from the luggage hold and set off for the hotel. Lucie worked as a chef in Hotel Bellini on Corso Vittorio Emanuele. It was a straight walk ahead, and she was looking forward to the exercise after all that time sitting on the bus. The traffic was extremely noisy and before long that, combined with the suffocating heat, made her incredibly thirsty. There was a juice bar up ahead so she stopped. Looking at the baskets of brightly colored summer fruit stacked around the tiny bar it was hard to decide, finally Susan decided on a pomegranate juice. The proprietor handed it over with a friendly smile and she drank in down eagerly.

She immediately felt revitalised and after a quick 'grazie' continued on her way up the street. Finally, the hotel came into sight. Hotel Bellini was a five -star establishment. An impressive façade was the first thing guests saw when they arrived, and the reception area continued through, building on the luxurious theme. There were brocade curtains in deep reds and greens, beautiful wall papers accented with gilt, welcoming soft lounges with low tables, urns holding brilliantly coloured flower arrangements and topped off with an amazing tiled floor. This all added to the first and lasting impression of this iconic, landmark hotel. Susan went up to the reception desk and let the woman on duty know she was meeting someone, then went and sat on one of the settees in the lounge area and messaged Lucie. It was nice sitting there in the air conditioned room, watching guests coming and going. Because it was peak holiday season it was incredibly busy. After about fifteen minutes Lucie appeared, she looked hot and harried in her black and white checkered chef's uniform. Sitting down, she gave Susan a quick kiss on both cheeks. 'Ciao, cara,' she said. 'It's a nightmare in the kitchen today, short staffed, late market deliveries Aaah! I shall go mad before the day is over, some of those people are so stupid, but what can I do.' She threw her hands up in exasperation.

Some things never changed, Susan thought, as she offered words of comfort. Lucie thrived on the chaos of the kitchen and Susan knew it. It was all part of the image and the job. 'I will be finished here at about ten-thirty and it's now nearly five, do you want to meet back here and then go back to Bagheria together? Is there something you can do until I finish? Maybe you could just rest here, I'm sure it will be ok if you want to do that.'

'That sounds good, I have to call in and see Commissario Lombardo at the Questura, so that will give me enough time hopefully.'

'I'd better go back now,' Lucie said, as she got up, 'before they ruin all the dinner preps. I'll take your case and put it in the luggage locker. Ciao, see you at ten-thirty,' and she was gone, taking the case with her.

Susan sat for a little longer before messaging the commissario, a message pinged back almost immediately. I'm at the office now, it said, message me when you get to reception and I'll come down. A map appeared soon after with directions, showing her the way.

Chapter 11

It didn't take long to get there and Susan arrived at the Questura in Piazza della Victoria in twenty minutes. After giving her name at the reception the commissario came almost immediately. He looked tired, but still managed a smile when he saw her.

'How are you Signora Susan?' he said, as he shook her hand.

'Fine, thanks.'

'My office is just upstairs, would you like a drink, water, coffee?' He asked as they walked up to the floor above.

'A water would be nice, thank you,' Susan replied.

He opened a door along the corridor and went inside. There was a uniformed officer on duty at the desk in the outer office. 'Can you bring two bottles of water, Santo, please,' he then opened the inner door. 'Come in and take a seat,' he pulled over a chair closer to the desk and then sat down on the other side, looking at her, an expression of concern on his face.

'How are you really, Signora Susan?'

'Well, to be honest, I'm feeling a little puzzled about everything. Have you managed to find Angela yet?'

'No, not yet, but I do have people working on it. We've been keeping a close eye on a few people here in Palermo, to see if they lead us anywhere.

Now, on top of everything else, a body was found last night down at the docks. A person, who we believe, is involved in people smuggling, but so far we haven't been able to find a motive... yet.'

The most disturbing thing about this death had been that when Lombardo had got to the docks and was able to look carefully at the body, which was floating between two fishing trawlers, tangled in nets and lobster pots, he had recognised the person straight away. It was Doni, Jonno's friend, who had organised, according to Rose, the job that Jonno had told her was waiting for him in Catania.

Susan, shocked by the news of yet another death, then preceded to tell the commissario about Aurelio's strange behaviour a few days ago, and his meeting later on with the man at the bus stop in Taormina. She then continued to fill him in with the recent events on the bus during her journey to Palermo. The sudden and inexplicable abduction of a passenger by two men at the road stop. How no one tried to help, and the feeling of helplessness that she had felt watching it all unfold in front of her. She finished her story by telling the commissario of the several strange coincidences related to this story. That the man she had seen at the bus stop in Taormina, talking to Aurelio and then driving him away in a car not long afterwards, was also one of the African bus passenger's abductors. 'It was the man from the mug shot, you know, from the folders I looked through with you in Taormina. It was definitely him. Gianni, isn't that his name?'

Lombardo listened quietly without commenting, a concerned look on his face. When Susan finished, ending with a description of how the man had been bundled into a car which had then sped off in the direction of Palermo, he finally spoke. 'I'm so sorry you were caught up in more violence, these things seem to be following you. I'll put out an alert, but I don't like our chances of finding out much. People are too frightened to get involved, so we just have to wait and hope some information comes through. The fact that we know Gianni is involved might make things a little easier, plenty of people know him but they are also frightened of him. He's a really nasty customer!'

'The car was dark blue, but I couldn't see even a part of the number plate,' Susan offered, feeling that she hadn't been observant enough.

'It was a shock,' she continued, 'you don't expect to see something like that at a bus stop in the middle of nowhere.'

'You can't blame yourself, it would have been too dangerous to do anything that would draw attention to you. They must have been following the bus, waiting for a chance to make a move before it got to Palermo. It would have been much harder to abduct someone from the terminus.'

The silence was broken by the shrill ring of his phone. 'Pronto,' he answered. 'Ah, ok I'll come straight way.' He put his phone in his pocket and got up. 'I have to go, someone's come in with some information about the abduction... that was quick.'

Susan walked down the stairs with him and after making sure she would let him know if anything came up, she said goodbye. As she was making her way towards the entrance, she noticed a small, weasel faced man looking furtively around him, as he waited near the reception desk. Walking back to the hotel. Susan saw that it was only eight-thirty. She suddenly felt hungry. Good, there was still time to have dinner.

Lucie came into the foyer where Susan was waiting. She had only been there for ten minutes. The timing was perfect. Lucie looked a lot calmer than when they had met earlier.

'How was your evening? Did you see the Commissario? Any news?'

Susan tried to answer the questions as best she could, but really there was not much that was new, unless you took into account the death of that poor thing down at the docks. How that fitted in with everything that was going on was impossible to know at this stage.

Thankfully, there was a train waiting at the station and they were home in Bagheria in no time. It was too late to stay up so they promised to have a really good catch up in the morning. Lucie didn't have to start work until the afternoon.

Susan slept deeply and awoke to the smell of freshly made coffee. Lucie was sitting on the terrace, the moka pot in front of her. The view was beautiful. Over the tops of roofs, you could see a glimpse of the sea. The sky was a deep, clear blue, and the air full of an early morning crispness. It wouldn't stay like that for long, in a few hours that crispness would have gone, replaced by the relentless heat of the Sicilian summer.

'How did you sleep?' Lucie asked.

'Like a log.' Lucie laughed at Susan's very Australian response.

They sat together sharing news about their respective children and grandchildren. 'Have you been to Malta this year?' Susan asked.

'No, not this year, I'll go over at Christmas. There have been so many expenses, what with the last lot of school fees and everything else that goes with them. I have some leave due then, so that's when I'll go.' Lucie looked sad as she spoke about this enforced, endless, separation between she and her husband. What a horrible situation, but the alternative was far worse. A bullet in the back of the head, when he least expected it, and then the repercussions that would certainly follow. Instead all they could hope for was that sometime in the distant future the slighted person would pass away, someone would take pity on them, and the debt would finally be repaid. After finishing their coffees, they decided to walk down to the beach, the sea air and exercise an added bonus to the rare time they were able to spend together. The beach was busy with family groups already staking a claim to a patch of sand, putting up their umbrellas and beach chairs. Children stood impatiently while parents coated them with sun block, squashing sun hats down on their heads, before they ran quickly into the shallow water, shrieking with screams of excitement. A few people walked along the shore, taking advantage of the cooler air to complete their daily exercise. Susan and Lucie decided to walk too. Down at the furthest end of the beach there was a small café, they sat down in the shade and drank a juice, gazing out to sea.

'How hopeless their futures must be, for people to leave everything behind and set sail in unsafe boats to an unknown future.' Susan's eyes were focused on the huge expanse of water in front of her. It stretched far away to the horizon.

'Facing uncertainty and danger would be a deterrent to all but the most desperate, I'm sure,' Lucie added. After sitting peacefully for a while, they reluctantly got up and began their walk home.

They had only been back for an hour when Lucie got a phone call from work telling her that one of her staff was ill and couldn't come in. 'So much for a relaxing afternoon,' she complained disappointedly.

Now faced with the prospect of a free afternoon, Susan decided to catch the train to Palermo with Lucie and then take the Hop-On, Hop-Off bus tour to Monreale. She hadn't been there for a few years and it would be a good chance to visit the cathedral again.

They walked down Via Maqueda together before parting ways, Lucie continuing further down to the hotel and Susan to the bus stop near Quattro Canti. Luckily there was a bus already there. She climbed on board, paid for her ticket and then went further up the next flight of steps to sit in the open air of the rooftop. It was already crowded with tourists from all over the world, sitting ready for the journey, their earphones turned to the language in which they would be following the tour.

The bus began its winding journey through the streets, past the docks and into areas of the city Susan was not familiar with. The buildings looked newer and the shops very basic, obviously not catering to the tourist trade. These were new workers' suburbs, hastily built apartment buildings, colourless, and lacking the sense of vibrancy found in the older, historic suburbs that Susan was more familiar with. They left the drab streets and drove on into almost countryside. Suddenly the bus pulled into a side parking area off the road, the tour guide announcing, 'we are visiting Castello della Zisa, we will be staying here for an hour and a half.' This was interesting because this stop had not been mentioned at the beginning of the tour. There was no choice but to get off the bus and join the other tourists walking over to a large building with the distinctive features particular to Islamic architecture. It was incredibly hot and there was not one bit of shade. Susan immediately thought of her half bottle of water that would have to keep her going for at least a few hours. When they finally reached the building, they found that there was an admittance charge of six euros. This caused a further delay as there was no change and people had to pay with a card if they didn't have the right money. Everyone started to look a bit frazzled, and when they were finally able to enter the castello, made a bee line for the inner rooms. The coolness of the stone walls was a welcome relief from the heat outside. Once inside, you had to follow a narrow stone staircase to each floor and on each floor were displays of artifacts. The slightly claustrophobic atmosphere made Susan feel uncomfortable and she started to long for the outdoors. Unfortunately, you appeared to only be able to go one way, and so she had to continue round and round the rooms. She was unable to take in much of the tour guide's commentary, and could only nod and smile in a feigned appreciation of what she was saying. Eventually she reached the end and thankfully almost leapt down the staircase until she reached the ground floor. To her utter confusion she found that she was still stuck inside the building and that to reach the outside she still had to look in a series of rooms which were filled with amazing mosaics and faded frescos. Susan had to admit, despite her growing frustration, that the beautifully patterned, tiled floors of the rooms were incredible, and feeling slightly ashamed of her earlier lack of interest, she took several photos with her phone.

Once outside, she sat thankfully in the coolness and noticed that she wasn't alone, many of the other people on the tour had also found seats around the building. After thirty minutes everyone started making their way back to where the bus was due to pick them up, but when they reached the designated stop the bus was nowhere to be seen. A slight feeling of panic hit Susan although the others didn't seem at all concerned.

I mustn't let them out of my sight, she thought. Imagine being stuck here in the middle of nowhere. She sat on the edge of a low stone wall with one eye looking out for the bus and the other keeping watch on what the others were doing. Finally, it appeared down the road and she waited, glad to get on board. Once on the bus, things suddenly took a turn for the worse, another group of people had joined the tour and were now also travelling on the bus. The seats previously taken by Susan's group had now been taken by others. Searching for a spare seat was becoming difficult. A very tall man in shorts, long socks and sandals, with a strong German accent, started yelling angrily. The tour guide tried to reason with him, but he kept on and on. Finally, he was given a seat down the back near a door where he could stretch his long legs without inconveniencing anyone. This move however, added to his increasingly bad temper as the door would occasionally open and shut, causing him to have to move his legs out of its way. Susan felt upset too as she had lost her comfortable seat and now sat squashed between a woman and two small children. The ride to Monreale stretched ahead with almost unbearable discomfort. After the unexpected stop at Castello della Zisa, the oppressive heat, wriggling children and the crowded bus added further to Susan's strong feeling that she had made the wrong choice for this day's activity.

As she stared out of the window the bus passed a small newspaper kiosk, papers were stacked outside with some of the later editions displayed on stands. From one of them a familiar face gazed out from underneath a large headline in bold, black type. Susan could understand the words, *persona scomparsa,* missing person.

Chapter 12

Coming down the worn marble stairs, Lombardo saw Gino standing in the shadows at the side of the staircase, his red-rimmed eyes looking furtively around him.

'Hey, what do you want Gino?'

'Ah Commissario, I've got a bit of news,' his wheedling voice slipping and sliding all over the place, his eyes failing to meet those of the policeman.

'Yes, what is it then? I'm busy, hurry up, out with it, don't waste my time!'

'I was wondering if you could you give me a bit of help sir? Work's been slow and the kids are crying out for new shoes and a trip to the seaside, just a bit, that's all I ask, just a bit....... please sir.'

'Give me what you've got, and I'll think about it, come on!'

'Well.... I was over at my cousins last night, you know, he lives near the docks, he's got a small bar. We were having a quiet drink with a few mates. Anyway, I went outside to have a cigarette. They don't allow smoking in there, health regulations, you can get fined. A stupid rule, if you ask me.'

'Alright, alright, get to the point!' Lombardo snapped at him.

'Ok, well I was just standing there looking at the lights over the water, when suddenly this car drives up. I pretended not to look, turned my head away, but I could see who they were, two of Don S's men, I'd recognise them anywhere, nasty buggers. So the car stopped and they both got out and opened the boot. I couldn't see what they took out because it was a bit far away. It looked like a person though, tied up or twisted in some way and his head was covered. As I looked away there was a shot, just one, followed by a splash. Oddio! I got rid of that cigarette quick smart and went straight back inside. I was shaking like you wouldn't believe, didn't say anything to anyone, just kept quiet, the fewer people know the better.'

Gino finally drew breath and looked at Lombardo.

'That's all I know but it's pretty significant, isn't it? Worth something I'd say.'

'Yes, it is interesting,' said the commissario. 'It makes sense I suppose. Well yes, you did well Gino,' and he took fifty euros from his wallet.

Gino quickly took the money and made to leave. 'Hold on,' and he called him back.

'There's something else that's happened and I want you to keep your sharp ears and eyes open. Someone was abducted from the Modica- Palermo bus, yesterday. From the description we were given I'd say it was Jonno, and now after what's happened to Doni I'm really concerned. I have a bad feeling about this. Just see if anyone has seen Jonno, and if they have, let me know straight away.'

'Sure thing,' Gino looked rattled by this news and made a beeline for the door.

'Don't forget I'll want to talk to you again soon,' Lombardo called after him.

Back in his office he sat down, pulling out a file from the top drawer. He started reading some notes while looking at several photos. One was of the dead African boy pulled from the docks the night before. His young face barely past that of a teenager, it was such a waste of a life. There were several other photos, faces set out on the desk like a suit of cards, hardened features, cruel eyes, and mouths. Men who would do what they were ordered to do without a second thought. A few threads were beginning to come together, but there was still a way to go before he would have enough evidence to bring people in for questioning. It was painstaking work, confusing and messy, trying to link people of interest to the crimes. They were often shadowy figures masquerading as pillars of the community, living a double life. Their enforcers' could be arrested easily, but a clever lawyer and powerful connections usually got them off. If, for some reason they had to serve any time, their families were looked after and their jobs would be still waiting when they got out. But, it was the others, the powerful ones hiding behind facades of respectability, who always managed to slip away..... they were the ones Lombardo was after, and he was determined to bring them to justice.

After shutting the file, Lombardo got up from his desk, took the file, and left the room. 'I'm just going out for a while Roberto, over to Terrasini,' he said to the officer sitting in the outer office. 'I'll take the car. I should only be gone for an hour or two.'

As he drove down the wide highway towards Terrasini, he thought of the man he was going to see. Don Vicenzu Saconne was *il capo* the head of an old and very powerful family, at least they had been powerful. Lombardo had heard on the grapevine that there had been a bit of trouble in the Saconne family recently. Younger family members, not happy with the old way of running things, had started asserting themselves, resulting in a bit of muscle-flexing and chest beating.

A chat with the patriarch might be worthwhile. The men Gino had seen at the docks were two of the enforcers from this family, but before pulling anyone in, the commissario wanted to first get Don Saconne's take on what had happened. He just hoped he would be forthcoming.

Things were changing and not for the good. In the past you knew who you were dealing with and things were more straightforward, but now, the sons of these dons had law degrees or economic degrees and were involved in more sophisticated and complex crimes. They didn't share the same belief in family honour or the importance of respect. Now, there was a ruthlessness that was new, and decidedly unpleasant.

Huge iron gates with an elaborate crest of a rearing leopard, displayed on the front, were the first in a number of barriers you had to pass through to enter this fortress. Lombardo rolled down his window and a barking command came over an intercom placed into the wall at face level. He stated his name, then told the disembodied voice that he wanted to speak with Don Saconne if he was available.

He'd enjoyed a fairly respectful relationship with the don, as much as was possible between a policeman and a mafia don, so he didn't think there would be a problem turning up without an appointment. After a few minutes, a squawking reply came back and the gates swung open. Turning into the long winding driveway he could see a couple of sentries standing on top of a wall and he knew a firearm would not be far away. There were also several security cameras placed along the drive. God! This place is a fortress, he thought to himself as he flashed his badge at the men, they waved him on.

The house up ahead was huge. A sandstone terrace with carved balustrades ran along one side and a massive door took up a large part of the front wall. Huge urns filled with brightly coloured flowers flanked the steps leading up to the door. Before Lombardo could even ring the bell the door opened and a man in a well-cut, expensive-looking suit stood there.

Putting out his hand, he greeted Lombardo with an oily smile.

'Welcome, it's an honour to have you here Commissario.'

Shaking his hand, he continued in an unpleasant fawning voice, 'I'm Lorenzo Butelli, Don Saconne's lawyer, he's in his office, let me take you there now.' He guided the commissario to an open door further up a long passageway. With a nod of his head, Lombardo briefly acknowledged the man he recognized as someone he had crossed paths with before. A slippery defense lawyer who represented some of the criminals Lombardo and his men had brought to court. A trickster with a very dubious reputation.

The lawyer stood back and the commissario walked through into a large study.

A portly man with enormous grey bushy eyebrows and a shock of thick hair which had been coloured a dark chestnut, sat on a throne-like chair behind a sparsely covered desk. A notebook, and what looked to be a thick diary, was all that Lombardo could see.

'It's good to see you Commissario,' the corpulent gentleman said, rising and gripping his hand firmly. 'How fortuitous that you came today, I was thinking of phoning you and making an appointment to meet you, but here you are.'

He let go of the commissario's hand and pointed to seat in front of the desk. 'Sit, sit. Would you like a coffee or another type of refreshment?'

Lombardo sat, declining the offer. 'No thank you, Don Saconne, I can't stay too long. I've come to talk to you about some disturbing things that have happened recently, here in

Palermo and over in Taormina as well. I know you have an ear to the ground and that nothing much escapes you, so I wondered if you could shed any light on the reasons behind these awful crimes. I'm talking mainly about the refugees who were massacred in Taormina and the death of an African at the docks in Palermo. I'm certainly not saying you had anything to do with them,' he added, as he saw a slight frown and the beginnings of an expression of refutation on Don Saconne's reddening face. The don looked less angry after those calming words and regarded Lombardo carefully before he began to speak.

'These are difficult times Commissario, business is not as good as it once was and there are certain groups who have been encroaching on the livelihoods of others.'

He gave a small smile and continued.

'They show no respect for our code and display very poor manners. They are rude and aggressive. Once, young people would never have behaved like that. My generation respected and listened to our elders. We learned from them and knew our place. These young pups today have had the opportunity of an education my generation never had. We worked hard to carve out our businesses, using our brains, tenacity, and connections. Now, these young ones think they are like gods, invincible and untouchable. They invest in businesses that are disreputable and cause extreme hardship to others. They are tarnishing our family name, our reputation.... We've always believed we were there to help the people who worked for us, to look after them. They are our responsibility.'

Lombardo looked slightly bemused after listening to these impassioned words. He had never thought of the mafia as a benevolent society. Any generosity or empathy was shown only if it worked in their favour. Maybe the rumours that Don

Saconne was showing early signs of dementia had some truth behind them.

He continued, 'I have to say, that what has been going on recently has disturbed me greatly, but my generation seems powerless to do anything to stop it. I can see that these youngsters are out of control. They have joined forces with people I would never have had anything to do with. Men who come from far away and don't share our values. There is now a blood feud between some of the families, stirred up by those strangers, putting ideas into the heads of our young ones. It makes them impatient and gives them false ideas of how powerful they can become. Telling them there is no need to wait, that they should take the opportunities that come their way now, not to ask for advice from their elders or wait their turn to become leaders. That fire is being fueled by those outsiders who come to our country from parts of the world we would once never have had anything to do with. Now, all we can do is sit, and wait, and hope that they don't decide that it is in their best interests to get rid of us.'

At the end of the unexpected outburst, Don Saconne sat back in his chair, exhausted.

His face had got even redder and he looked unwell. As he tried to calm him, Lombardo considered the age of Don Saconne. He must be getting on in years, middle to late eighties, Lombardo thought.

He had to admit, that after years of interacting with these crime families, he did have an uneasy respect for this old school mafia don. It was certainly true; the younger generation was different. Entitled, with no compassion or sense of responsibility, they certainly were harder to deal with.

After the don had calmed down sufficiently, Lombardo continued the conversation.

'So what you are saying is a group of young men are trying to outdo each other, and people are dying because of it? So what have you got to say about a report that has landed on my desk, putting two of your men in a car with a man who was later found dead with a bullet in the back of his head, floating in the water down at the docks?

Do you know anything about that?'

'No! I don't!' Don Saconne's face became redder and he hastily grabbed at a glass of water. Lorenzo Butelli, who must have been waiting just outside the door came quickly into the room. 'It's alright,' the don said, waving him away. His colour slowly returning to normal, he continued, 'I no longer know what is going on, people don't tell me things anymore. They think it will harm my health, so most of the time I have to find out from other sources.'

There definitely was a problem, and once again, it was the same issues which reappeared time and time again. Arresting the small fry who could easily be replaced was not the answer. Finding the middlemen was a little better, but to get to the people who sat at the top of these businesses was almost impossible. Buried in red tape and bureaucratic government departments, tangled up in legal loopholes made going after these people a nightmare. Lombardo thought briefly of all the others who had tried before him. Often falling victim to assassinations or illness caused by the relentless stress of trying to seek justice. Sometimes the head of one of those mafia families, along with their businesses was brought down, often after years of patiently following trails, as well as a certain amount of good luck. When it had happened, the average person in the street rejoiced, but it didn't happen often enough and the pain and suffering these people caused was far greater than a one in a thousand good result. Don Saconne looked exhausted after that coughing fit and Lombardo knew he wouldn't be getting any more information now.

He got up and said his goodbyes, feeling rather despondent as he walked back down to his car. What Don Saconne had said was true, this was a much harder situation to deal with and he wondered if he had the necessary energy and will power to keep going. He was going to have to think long and hard to work out what his next plan of action would be, starting with a long chat with the don's son, Peppino.

After the events of the last few days, and the fact that there was no sign of him at the house, Lombardo thought he was probably keeping out of his father's way. It was hard to know where he could be, there were so many possibilities. The best thing to do at this point was to go back to Palermo and keep working from there. Turning the car around, he drove slowly back down the driveway, barely glancing at the sentries stationed along the way. He didn't know if the visit had been worth it. Hopefully, someone would put the word out and Peppino would make a move. He had stirred the serpents nest now all he could do was wait. Peppino would certainly want to know the reasons behind his visit and what he had told his father. It was also highly likely he would want to know what his father had told the commissario.

Chapter 13

A thin sliver of blue between the slats of the wooden shutters was the only thing visible outside the room. Angela reluctantly pulled herself away and sat back down on the bed, pondering her fate. She had been locked in this room for at least twelve hours.

She knew she was on the island of Levanzo, after being grabbed while she was walking along a path in Savoca. The abduction had come out of the blue, she hadn't even known she was being watched or that anyone had been aware that she had left Taormina and gone to Savoca to stay with her aunt. All she knew, was that a car had suddenly stopped, blocking her way as she was out walking, getting some much needed fresh air and exercise. A man had got out quickly, and before she had time to react had pulled her into the back of the car.

A black hood was dragged roughly over her head, and then she was pushed down on the back seat. She remembered the long journey vividly. The twisting and turning of winding roads taking her across the rugged Sicilian mountains. Her throat was parched from the lack of air in the closed space of the claustrophobic hood. After constant pleas, she was finally given water to quench her unbearable thirst. When they had finally stopped, she felt the car being driven on to a ferry and then the choppy ride over to an island. The men who had brought her here had not been rough, or disrespectful, but neither had there been any kindness or real concern for her welfare. It was as if she was a parcel being delivered to someone.

Angela realised, not long after she had been locked in this room that she was in Aurelio's cousin's family house. What she didn't know was why.

She had been in this house a year ago with Aurelio. It was someone's birthday party and she had been really excited about going there. The family was incredibly rich and the house was glorious. Built, using white stone quarried from the area, the villa had huge verandahs and its large windows were closed against the sun with brilliant blue shutters. It perched high on a cliff overlooking the Mediterranean Sea. A fast luxurious boat had delivered she and Aurelio, plus a handful of other university friends, to a wharf at the bottom of the cliffs. She remembered the brightly coloured fishing boats in the small harbour, and the long climb from the wharf up a zigzagging flight of steps that had been carved out of the side of the cliff. When they reached the top there were beautiful gardens and a rolling green lawn. Dotted here and there were terraces filled with pots of bougainvillea and other plants and flowers. She had gasped with pleasure, whilst taking in the wonderful scene. Around a landscaped pool were groups of people, the beautiful people. European jet setters, movie stars, artists, and musicians. She recognised an opera singer and several movie stars who had been in Taormina for the annual film festival. They were chatting in groups, drinking an assortment of brightly coloured cocktails and a local prosecco, whilst helping themselves to a selection of food from enormous platters of antipasti. Angela also saw several people who were business associates of her father. Some of the younger people she recognised as former classmates from school, but she no longer moved in those circles, preferring university life. Study and working for social change. The aimless life of these people did not interest her at all.

The party had dragged on and on. Peppino, who had drunk too much and snorted too much coke, started fights with several guests. These altercations appeared to have been driven by a mixture of excess alcohol and drug-induced paranoia. The climax came when he drew a gun and started firing at people he believed to be undercover police. The family's security had overpowered him and he was taken away to calm down. It was a nightmare and she was glad when Aurelio decided it was time to leave.

Now, here she was, locked in a room with no idea of why she was there. After the two men had taken her to this prison-like bedroom, they had removed the hood. Soon after, a maid had unlocked the door and brought in a jug of water and a panino, leaving them on a small table. She had neither spoken nor looked at Angela, coming and going without raising her eyes. Angela had eaten hungrily before falling into an uneasy sleep. Now it was morning, she had showered and was sitting waiting for someone to come and tell her why she was here. Was it something to do with what had happened in Taormina, something to do with Peppino and Aurelio or their family? Did it have anything to do with that family meeting she had found out about when she read the message on Aurelio's phone? She didn't feel particularly frightened, just puzzled, and she knew that when her father found out about this he was not going to happy with whoever had been responsible for abducting his precious daughter.

After thirty minutes she heard the door being unlocked and the same maid from yesterday came in carrying a cup of coffee, some water and a plate of pastries.

After putting them down, she finally spoke in a soft voice, heavy in local dialect. 'Please eat, the young master will see you after you have eaten. I'll come back and take you to him.'

The food and coffee made her feel a million times better. Now she felt strong and ready to deal with whatever happened next.

Following the maid down a long corridor and out on to one of the terraces, Angela saw two men standing together, deep in conversation, coffee cups in their hands. They were dressed in similar outfits, soft cream shirts, and dark linen pants, both in their thirties, with tanned, athletic bodies. There was a third man with them, older and fat, he looked dishevelled and sweaty and seemed to be more of an employee judging by the way he kept his distance and was listening, rather than talking. One of the men seemed preoccupied with a stream of messages coming through on his phone... taking little notice of the other who was trying to engage with him in a passionate conversation. Two of the men turned as Angela walked towards them, she recognised Peppino straight away. The other remained still focused on his phone. The sweaty, fat man glanced at her briefly then turned his attention to the table of food, set out for breakfast, in the corner of the terrace. As she got closer Angela couldn't get over how much he looked like Aurelio, they could have been twins, except where Aurelio had an open honest face, Peppino's was cruel, his eyes were cold and devoid of kindness.

He came towards her, putting his hand proprietorially on her arm.

'Angela, how are you feeling, did you sleep well?'

He drew her closer to him and looked steadily into her eyes. He sounded so insincere, Angela felt like slapping him.

'Sorry about this, but we didn't have a choice. It's about a business proposition I have for your father. I haven't contacted him yet, I want him to stew for a bit, before I get in touch. I know he loves you so much and now that you are missing he will be out of his mind with worry, and your mother...... I can't imagine what she will be going through.

You're here in case he has a problem agreeing to our terms. You could say, as a sort of insurance, to help him make the right choice. I know how precious you are to him, so hopefully, bringing you here to stay with us will be an added incentive to convince him to join with us. If not, I'm afraid things could get very bad, especially for you. No one wants that to happen, certainly not me. I might get your friend, my dear cousin Aurelio, to speak to your father on our behalf as well. We'll see how fond of you he really is, and how concerned for your welfare.'

He continued to look at her, his cold eyes unwavering in their stare.

'You'll have to stay here until an agreement has been reached, however long it takes. I hope for your sake it happens sooner rather than later. We have people who are impatient for an answer and they are not as tolerant as us.'

'So I am meant to stay here, while you sort out your family business problems? It seems a bit desperate Peppino, don't you think?' Angela looked at him thoughtfully. 'What about your father? What does he think? Is he involved too? He and my father are good friends; I can't imagine Don Saconne permitting my abduction. You have no idea what this will do to my father. I wouldn't want to be on the receiving end of his anger and retribution when he finds out what you have done. Have you really thought this through, about what you are doing?'

'Dear Angela, I don't have any choice. I need your father's bank; I've run out of options. Do you think I would have put you through all this if there was another way?

Anyway my father's past it. They're both past it, yours and mine.

I'm working on my own this time. It's my chance to prove I'm ready to be the don. What do they know of how the modern world works now?

The old ways of doing things just don't work anymore. Things have changed, he's living in the past, and very soon he will realise that I have to run things now. It's time for the young blood to take over from those dinosaurs.

You know, Angela, I'm so sick of waiting. I'm sick of having to run things by him all the time, only having them knocked on the head before I've even finished explaining. He's become too timid in his old age, lost his fight, too locked into the old ways of doing things.

His generation is finished, if only they could see that and give us a chance instead of fobbing us off with odd jobs. I've built up networks all over the world. Those people are just waiting for a chance to get into our new business ventures. With him, it's just the same old, same old.'

Angela stood waiting for him to finish. He seemed unstable, and she didn't want to do anything to make him even angrier, so she kept quiet, waiting for him to stop. After a while, he became calmer.

'Sorry, Angela, we have to keep you here for a while longer. I promise you'll be comfortable and well looked after. You'll be here for maybe a week, less if certain people agree to meet our demands.'

He then turned his attention to the fat man. 'Gianni, I want you to pay my father a visit. Take one of the other men with you as well. I want you to deliver a message,' and he handed him an envelope. 'You don't have to wait for an answer. I'm sure he'll contact me soon enough, after he's read what I have to say. Now go, I have to make a few phone calls.' After the dismissal, Gianni left the room, as he turned, Angela saw the handle of a handgun sticking out of his belt, and for the first time, she suddenly felt frightened and uncertain of her future. She began to wonder what would happen to her if Peppino's threats were not taken seriously enough. Her family must be looking for her, they would have contacted the police by now, surely. Her aunt would have been worried when she didn't return from her walk and rung her father straight away.

Peppino turned and walked out of the room followed by the other man, who Angela had not been introduced to. He still remained fixated on his phone. Peppino called back to her as he left.

'Maria will take you back to your room now, I'll get her to bring you some magazines, maybe they will help you while away the hours, there's also a TV if you feel like watching something. I'll speak to you later when I've had some news. Ciao.'

After Maria had once again locked the door, Angela sat and went over the conversation she had just had with Peppino. She had heard from Aurelio many times about his cousin's unstable behaviour and insatiable greed for power. It was common knowledge that over the past few years, there had been changes in the attitude of some of the sons of the most powerful families in Palermo, and other parts of Sicily. It was different now, education and the ability to travel easily around the world had opened doors to a wealth of experiences, and contact with different types of people. Now the old order was being challenged by the new.

If only there was a way of contacting her father, or Aurelio.

Maybe I could work on Maria, she must have a phone. If I appeal to her, girl to girl, she might take pity on me, or I could offer her something....

Angela decided to turn on the TV and see if there was any news. After a few overseas news stories, she suddenly saw a photo of herself, listed as a missing person. The story shifted to her father talking to a reporter and appealing for news of his daughter. He looked stressed and confused. Angela began to cry. She turned the TV off again. What was the good of watching that? It wasn't going to do anything to help her situation, it was only making her feel worse. She had to think of a way to contact someone. She wept again, a feeling of hopelessness sweeping over her. When Maria came in with her lunch she found her lying across the bed. She raised her tear-stained face to the maid. 'Please, please help me, Maria. I beg you, please help me.'

Chapter 14

The Hop-On, Hop-Off bus drew into the stop next to Piazza della Vittoria. Susan got down and gratefully stretched her cramped legs. The final leg of the tour to Monreale had been uncomfortable, and the walk around the famous Cattedrale di Monreale even more so. Hordes of tourists had descended on the tourist hot spot, and so, a quiet contemplative stroll had been out of the question. Lines of Chinese and Americans followed guides holding flags of their respective countries and spoke loudly to each other. Their jarring voices intruded on the tranquil beauty of the courtyard, driving Susan to finally find refuge in a quiet corner. There, she spent the remainder of the afternoon gazing at the shimmering mosaics and counting the minutes until the bus began the journey back to Palermo.

Checking her messages, Susan noticed there was a new one from Aurelio, how interesting. He said, that after asking around, discreetly, he now thought he had a good idea where Angela was, but he wanted to check first without drawing attention to what he was doing. He wondered if Susan would like to join him on a trip to Levanzo tomorrow. He could pretend to be her tour guide. She responded straight away with a yes. It was two years since she had visited the island and was happy to go back, especially if it could help to shed more light on what had happened to Angela.

Now all she wanted to do was have a long, cold drink and relax.

Lucie had finished work and was waiting for her at a small family trattoria near the station. After sharing a plate of antipasti, they settled on bowls of pappardelle coated with a delicious ragu. It was a specialty of the house, and after the first forkful, washed down with some full-bodied red wine, Susan began to feel the unpleasantness of the day become a distant memory.

Over dinner, Susan filled Lucie in about her day, finishing with the message she had received from Aurelio, and their planned trip to Levanzo tomorrow.

'Please be careful,' Lucie warned. 'Those people are dangerous and you don't know if Angela is there or not, it's just a hunch. Aurelio's young, and by all accounts a bit of a hothead and a daredevil. He's also a member of the Saconne family, never forget that. My husband had dealings with them and they are dangerous and unpredictable. Be very, very, careful, Susan. You don't know those people, or Sicilian life. Are you sure you've thought this through?'

Susan looked at her. 'I think I have, we are just going for a day trip. I'll act like a tourist and he will be my guide. He's going to take the car, so we won't be too exposed. I promise I'll be careful,' she added.

Lucie still didn't look convinced, but knew when she was beaten, and they finished their meal without mentioning it again.

The next day Aurelio was waiting for her in the Palermo train and bus terminus car park. Before she left, Susan had promised Lucie she would stay in touch throughout the day, and they parted with a hug.

It didn't take long before they had left the city and were on the way to Trapani where they would catch the car ferry over to Levanzo. Aurelio started filling Susan in on what he had found out over the last couple of days. After he had finished rattling on about the Saconne family problems, Susan jumped in quickly. Several things had been puzzling her, and she felt she needed an explanation.

'Aurelio, do you mind telling me what happened that day at the bus terminus in Taormina?' Susan asked.

'Why was that man you were talking to so angry? Afterwards I saw you in a car, and he was driving. Where were you going?

I found it a bit strange because I recognised him. His photo was in a folder of mug shots I looked through with the commissario. I also saw him having an argument with an African man near a restaurant while I was having dinner. He, and another man, who's photo was also in the commissario's folder. Later, the same African was lying in the street with a knife sticking out of him. You knew all about that. Why aren't you telling me the truth? The whole thing seems incredibly dodgy to me.

Furthermore, just where do you fit in Aurelio? Whose side are you on? If there are sides. I agreed to come with you because I feel a sense of responsibility towards Angela and to those poor murdered people on Isola Bella as well. You need to give me some answers, that's only fair, if you want me to be part of your 'reconnaissance'.' She looked at him expectantly.

Oh! I didn't mean to do that, Susan thought to herself. That was a bit silly, she was shocked by the force of her accusations and also a little scared. It was true, she didn't really know him. Lucie's warnings were now uttermost in her mind.

'Sorry, Aurelio, I didn't mean to sound like an inquisitor,' and she gave him a little smile. 'I'm just curious, I'm sure you understand, but if you'd rather not talk about it, that's fine too.'

'It's ok Susan, don't be sorry. I can understand your curiosity and I know you are concerned about Angela. It's just that things are so complicated in my family. You must know that. I'm sure the commissario has told you a little about them. Like many stories in history here are two sides to my family. Good and evil, black and white, yin and yang..... My grandfather was a very powerful don. He built up and controlled many businesses here in Sicily. People loved him but at the same time they were frightened of him as well. He spent a lot of time in America after the Second World War, but eventually, things became too dangerous for him there. I believe he had trodden on a few too many toes, both on the right and wrong side of the law. So he moved back here permanently. He had two sons, my father Corrado, and Peppino's father Vicenzu. They both were given the same opportunities, but after finishing school they chose different paths. My father decided to use his family connections to do good. He was influenced by several judges and priests who wanted to lift people out of poverty and give them a chance to follow a life independent of the families who had controlled them for generations. He set up a foundation that pays for disadvantaged children's schooling, organised co-ops for farmers, where they can sell their produce for a decent price and get cheap loans so that they don't fall victim to loan sharks. It is the exact opposite of what his brother chose to do. My uncle is a criminal. Despite his wealth, his fancy house, and extensive business interests all over the world, the bottom line is that he is still a criminal. His drug business exploits children. He controls protection rackets under the guise of helping people, and makes huge amounts of money through loan sharking, and that's just a small part of it. Now that he's getting older he has mellowed slightly and isn't as ruthless as he once was. He and my father are even making an effort to reconnect in their twilight years. Their relationship is better than it has ever been and that drives my cousin mad. Peppino and his friends, some of whom are the sons and nephews of the patriarchs of these families, don't always agree with the way things are being done and want the chance to do it their way. They are involved in more sophisticated businesses and although they think they are cleverer and more modern thinking, their objectives are the same. To make money by exploiting vulnerable people.'

After that outburst, he was quiet. The road stretched ahead and they drove on in an uneasy silence. Aurelio suddenly slowed down. There was a turn off to Terrasini and Aurelio took it.

'I thought we were going to Trapani?' Susan said, looking at him.

'Seeing that sign and talking about my uncle made me think it might be a better idea to call in and see him before I go on to Trapani, he might have heard something and have a better idea of what's going on. You can meet him, and see what you think.'

That makes sense I suppose, Susan thought as they drove on. I wonder what this will be like? Although she had read books and watched films like The Godfather, she had never actually met a real don, not that she would have known if she had met one. In Sicily, it was hard to know, as the society functioned on so many different levels. Being a tourist, you wouldn't be aware anyway, unless someone told you, that is.... It would certainly be an interesting experience meeting Don Saconne.

Although Terrasini was a picturesque town on the coast famous for the breathtaking Capo Rama Natural Reserve, Susan also thought of it as being slightly sinister, because of its name. A shadowy crime figure in the Italian crime series from the eighties and nineties, La Piovre, The Octopus, also shared that name, and whenever she heard it, she thought of him.

Finally, they came to some tall iron gates and after Aurelio spoke into a security intercom, the gates opened and they drove through. The long driveway wound up a steep sunburnt hill, there were more hills ahead of them, undulating towards the horizon, hazy in the unrelenting summer sun. Tall trees lined either side and perched on a high stone wall ahead she could see guards with binoculars and guns at their sides, patrolling the perimeter of a palatial house. Terraces with terracotta urns full of tumbling, brightly coloured bougainvillea immediately caught Susan's eye. Over to one side was a citrus grove, fat, yellow lemons hung there like golden Christmas baubles. Further down was an olive grove, and far off in the distance what looked to be, a vineyard.

They drove up to an area that was a car park. Several expensive-looking cars were parked in a shaded area and Aurelio pulled into space nearby. As soon as he turned off the engine a man came down the stone steps leading from a terrace above. Although he wore a suit, by his demeanor Susan was sure he was a guard of some sort. The shape of a handgun was obvious beneath his jacket.

'Aurelio!' He looked happy to see him, greeting him warmly and grabbing his hand in a strong handshake.

'What are you doing here?

We've had a few visitors lately, Commissario Lombardo was here yesterday and now you and....' He looked at Susan intently, waiting for Aurelio to introduce them.

'Oh, this is Signora Susan, she's from Australia, on holiday here. Signora, this is Lorenzo, my uncle's lawyer. I've offered to take her to Levanzo for a bit of sightseeing, but when we were passing the Terrasini turnoff, I thought, as it was a while since I'd seen uncle, we'd drop in and say hello.'

'Pleased to meet you,' the lawyer said, shaking Susan's hand. She couldn't help thinking, as she returned the greeting, that the man, with his hooded, almost reptilian eyes did bear an uncanny resemblance to the Terrasini in the television show.

'He's been a bit down today. I think the commissario's visit yesterday, knocked him around emotionally. After he left he went back into his study and shut the door, saying he didn't want to be disturbed for the rest of the day. Your visit should brighten him up, I hope.'

Together, they walked up the long flight of steps leading to the main entrance and went on through the huge carved doors into a reception area. Susan stood for a moment taking in the size of the room. It was huge, with a high, ornately carved ceiling. The floor was covered with traditional, Sicilian hand- made tiles. The green, blue and yellow patterns spread out around her. Billowing sheer white curtains hung from floor to ceiling, the windows letting in some light which filled the room with a subdued golden glow. It was breathtaking!

Susan's first impression of Don Saconne was surprising. She had imagined he would look like some of the mafia dons she had seen portrayed in movies, slightly sinister and definitely in charge. Instead, she was greeted by a comical character from an Italian opera. Don Saconne was portly, with enormous grey eyebrows and a full head of luxuriant, chestnut brown hair. He gave Aurelio a big hug and then turned towards Susan, greeting her warmly. As she shook his hand Susan noticed a slight tremor in his grip. She let go gently and began to compliment him on his stunning home.

'It is truly a beautiful home, Don Saconne, the tiles are magnificent and I love the décor too. I feel honoured to have had the chance to visit it.'

He waved the words aside. 'Thank you, you are too kind, we just think of it as our family home. Saconnes have been here for many generations. Each one has added something over the years. It started as just a humble farmer's cottage and thanks to some good business choices it has grown into this, but we never forget the hardships and are grateful for what we have been able to achieve.'

Let's go into the sitting room and we can have a chat. It is quite a while since you last visited, Aurelio. I think I have seen more of your father; he has become a regular visitor over the last few months. Would you like a cool drink, some iced lemon water?' He rang a small bell and a maid came in straight away. 'A jug of iced lemon please Josie, and some of those delicious biscotti that Giovanna baked yesterday.'

After she had left the room they sat back in some incredibly comfortable armchairs and waited for someone to break the rather uneasy silence.

Aurelio was the first to speak. 'How is Peppino uncle, I haven't seen him in ages? And Sara how is she?'

Aurelio had filled Susan in earlier, on their way to the house, about various family members. Sara was Don Saconne's daughter. She had moved to Germany ten years ago, to study medicine. During her studies, she had met and married a German doctor and now lived there permanently. She visited every Christmas to see her father and that was all. She and her brother, Guiseppi, known by all as Peppino, were the only children of the marriage and had little to do with each other. Their mother, the don's wife, Laura had died over fifteen years ago after complications from diabetes. The house, despite its grandeur, was lonely and an air of sadness hung over it like an invisible pall. There were no sounds of happy grandchildren running down the corridors or out in the garden. There were just the staff and some of Don Saconne's hangers-on. So much for wealth and power. No wonder Peppino was impatiently waiting in the wings ready to take over. It made Susan feel sad.

'Oh Peppino, he comes and goes. He does his own thing. Sara is well, she has three children, two girls, and a boy. She comes every Christmas. It is such a joy to see them. They make my heart sing with joy. Their happy faces, such dear, dear children.'

'I was hoping to catch up with Peppino, is he at the house on Levanzo, or the apartment in Palermo?' Aurelio asked.

'The last I heard he was on Levanzo, but who knows. I'm usually the last to know. He only calls in if he wants some funds released. Sometimes he has a question he wants to ask Lorenzo or a problem he wants him to sort out.'

The don looked crestfallen, then quickly changed the subject, asking about Aurelio's criminology studies and they continued talking about the cases he was studying.

'We were actually on our way to Levanzo, before I decided to turn off, and see how you were. I want to show Susan the interesting parts of the island, like a tour guide,' Aurelio said, laughing.

'We'll take a chance and call in at the house anyway, on the off chance Peppino is there. I suppose we'd better go, uncle. It was great to see you.'

After saying their goodbyes, Susan and Aurelio got into the car and started driving away.

'Did you feel that was a bit awkward?' Susan said. 'He didn't seem to know what was going on. Poor man.'

'I wouldn't be wasting too much sympathy on him,' Aurelio smiled at her. 'He is a clever man and very cunning. He likes people to think he's helpless, but a lot of it is an act. He knows perfectly well what's going on, believe me.'

Lombardo had not been back at his desk for more than fifteen minutes when his deputy came into the office breathing heavily and sounding incredibly angry.

'Those bloody people, I can't believe it. This city is sitting on a powder keg, the slightest thing could set it off and this just might be it!'

'Calm down Stefano, what is it?'

His deputy stopped in front of his desk and took a deep breath. 'Those gangs, down at the docks, there's been another brawl. Many people were involved and innocent people were injured. They even went further into the Vucciria. Some tourists who were sitting having a quiet drink were caught up in the melee and knocked to the ground. One of them has a broken arm and they're all suffering from shock.'

'What started it? Have you found out yet?'

'Aah! Turf warfare, I gather, and retaliation for that poor thing they found the other night floating in the water with a bullet in his head. It's that migrant gang from Albergheria, the Nigerians, against the locals from La Kalsa, but I think somebody has been stirring it up from outside. This is the tourist season for heaven's sake! Our city has worked hard to put the past violence and its bad reputation behind it, and now this has happened.'

Albergheria, in particular the Mercato di Ballaro`, the market area, was once a mafia drug stronghold, but now much of the drug trade is shared with the Nigerians in an uneasy subordinate relationship. The mafia still being the ones in charge. It was commonplace for there to be bursts of antagonism between locals and the new arrivals, but killing someone with a trademark mafia hit was highly unusual.

'Have you arrested anyone yet?'

'Yes, we picked up a couple of them from each side. They're downstairs now. Do you want to speak to them or will I just deal with it.?'

'No, you deal with it, but if you can, see if anyone knows about Doni, in particular why he was killed?

And see if there's any word about Jonno. He and Doni were friends. The last I heard from his sister was that there was some work in Catania and Jonno had gone there. But after speaking to a witness to a kidnapping off the bus from Modica to Palermo the other day, the description given to us matches Jonno.

It makes the whole thing even more puzzling. If you can get anything out of them, it would be helpful. Any ideas any of them might have, but don't be too heavy handed. After I spoke to Don Saconne, I had the feeling that some of the young bloods have been stirring things up a bit. I think it could be one of two things, or even both. Drugs and smuggling.

I've also heard a few things about the prostitution business, which could be tied to the smuggling and the labour market. Could be someone treading on someone's toes.

Anyway, just ask a few questions without making too much of a thing about it. See what comes up and take note of the sort of responses you get, then get back to me later.'

The deputy went back downstairs and Lombardo continued to sit at his desk deep in thought. He really couldn't get those seemingly random events out of his head. Starting with the bodies in the boat in Taormina through to this afternoon's brawl, they were all connected somehow to Don Saconne and his son.

Down in the cells, groups of angry youths shouted insults through the bars at each other. 'Black Pig! Go back across the water to where you came from.'

'Shut up or I'll slit your bloody throat.'

The words bounced off the walls and echoed around them. A sergeant, looking incredibly fed up, greeted Stefano gratefully.

'Glad to see you, sir, this lot are driving me nuts, they're still stirred up. A night in the cells might just be the answer.

I reckon if we put them back outside it will start all over again. Their blood is really on the boil. A bunch of hotheaded young thugs, the lot of them, if you ask me.'

'Thanks, Marco, go and have a break for thirty minutes, I've got a few questions I want to ask them. Off you go.'

The sergeant went off quickly before he could change his mind.

'Right! Who wants to get out of here tonight?'

Stefano looked at the faces peering out at him from behind the bars.

'Not me, cop pig,' came the reply from the local gang's cell.

'Me either, dickhead!' Someone spat back from the Nigerian side.

'You don't even know what you have to do yet, so maybe listen first to what I have to say, without getting all steamed up.'

There was silence and he continued.......

'I want the answers to only two questions.

One, why are you fighting?

And two, what happened to Doni?'

The silence continued for a few minutes longer.

'Who's Doni?'

Someone from the La Kalsa side sniggered and another voice piped up.

'You mean the filthy scum from the docks?

The one shot in the head?

The one they found the other night?

He got what was coming, the greedy pig.'

'Shut your mouth, Sal.'

His friend in the cell gave him a shove.

'Keep your mouth shut, for bloody sake.'

Sal, a boy of about 17, with the beginnings of a soft moustache and an elaborate hairstyle, looked slightly sheepish, took his friend's advice, and didn't say another word. His friend stared back at Stefano with a defiant glare.

'We don't know anything.'

The Nigerians didn't say a word, just looked watchfully from behind the bars.

'Did you boys know him, Doni?' The deputy looked at them not expecting any response, and none was forthcoming.

'Ok I'll leave you to spend the night in the cells then. Maybe you'll change your minds if a few homeless drunks have to spend the night in here with you. They can smell pretty shocking, but I'm sure you'll get used to it. Sometimes they throw up, or piss their pants as well. Have a pleasant night boys,' and he started walking up the stairs.

'Hey!' A voice shouted from the Nigerian side. 'He didn't deserve what he got, he was ok.'

'Keep your mouth shut!' Several voices yelled out at once.

'Shut up! or Il Gattopardo will get you!'

Il Gattopardo? The Leopard? What sort of name was that...? The name of a famous book by Sicilian writer Guiseppi Tomasi di Lampedusa? The only book he wrote.

The deputy stopped and came back down.

'What was that?

What did you say?

Who's The Leopard?'

There was silence again, pairs of eyes peering warily from the cells.

'It's ok, just a joke.'

'It's an unusual name, that's all,' the deputy commented. 'What does this person do? With that name, he must be someone special, especially if he makes you so scared.

Did he have something to do with Doni's death?'

As no further conversation was forthcoming, Stefano left again, but now with a name to follow up.

'I've got a name,' Stefano said, as he came into Lombardo's office. 'It's not a real name, but it's a start. Il Gattopardo? Ever heard of anyone calling themselves that?'

'No,' replied Lombardo. 'Sounds a bit theatrical doesn't it. The Leopard, sort of old world,' he laughed. 'I've heard a few aliases, Horseface, Chicken Man, but that's a new one to me.

Maybe it's someone asserting their power, or a newcomer who's moved into the area and wants to make an impression. Anyway, I'll ask around and see if anyone 's heard the name before.'

'It seemed to make them scared when it was mentioned though, so it must be someone they're very frightened of. They told the person who mentioned it to shut up straight away,' Stefano said thoughtfully.

'Who used that name? Which side?'

'One of the La Kalsa boys, but he shut up pretty quickly. At first, I thought it had something to do with the drug trade at the

Mercato di Ballaro`. You know that uneasy alliance between the local mafia and the Nigerians? Well, now I think it's more than that. Something much bigger. A lucrative moneymaking business that someone doesn't want to lose control of, so they are frightening the opposition.'

'That sounds right,' Lombardo nodded.

'Should we leave those boys in overnight?' Stefano asked. 'If we release them now, whatever started this will flare up again, I have no doubt.'

'Yes, leave them there, it might make them think twice about brawling in public spaces and endangering people. Nothing more to do now, so go home, and spend some time with your family Stefano.'

After Stefano left, he sat back and made several phone calls.

The first was to Angela's father, Rocco Salvino. The phone rang for quite a long time before he answered. His voice sounded anxious. 'Hello, hello.'

Lombardo spoke quickly, 'it's Commissario Lombardo calling Mr. Salvino. I was wondering if you had heard from Angela, or any news about her?'

'No,' came the sad and frustrated reply. 'I haven't heard a thing. It's been nearly forty-eight hours.'

'No ransom demands, no threats?' Lombardo continued.

'No, nothing. I'm still wondering why she was taken? What could they want? I've spoken to Aurelio a few times but he hasn't heard anything either. Angela's mother is beside herself, she just lies on her bed crying. She's heartbroken and keeps saying, what if she never sees her again. It's unbelievable that anyone would take her like that.'

'I am still on it sir; I might have a lead, but I don't want to get your hopes up yet. Please tell your wife we are doing everything we can to find your daughter and bring her home. Stay strong, I'll be in touch,' and he hung up.

Lombardo hesitated for a few moments before he made the next call. A bit of a plan was needed before he spoke to Don Saconne.

The don answered almost immediately. 'Hello Don Saconne, it's Commissario Lombardo. I need to ask you a few questions. Are you free?'

'Yes, yes go ahead.' His voice wavered slightly.

Lombardo thought he sounded old and tired.

'Have you heard from Peppino? Has he visited the house today?'

'No, not today,' came back the prompt reply. 'He rang last week to check on a shipment of farm machinery we have coming in from Russia. He had mislaid the paperwork and wondered if I had a copy of the shipping details, which I did. I was expecting him to come to the house, we usually try to have dinner together once a week, but I haven't heard from him so far. Tell me, why is it important Commissario?'

'It's alright, don't worry yourself. ......by the way, where does he spend most of his time, if not with you at the house?'

'Well, he has the apartment in Palermo, you know, near the cathedral and I think he tries to spend time at the house on Levanzo, each weekend.'

Oh yes, the house on Levanzo, Lombardo had forgotten for a moment about that house. An impressive, clifftop villa on one of the Egadi Islands. He had heard rumours about the weekend parties that were held there, and the guests who attended them. A couple of officers from the Questura had gone there several times after two prostitutes were reported missing by their families. They were never found and their inquiries had stalled. No one from the party had been willing to talk, denying any knowledge that they had been there, so, without any evidence the police had never been able to prove what had happened to them, or that they had ever been there. The officers had returned to the Questura, frustrated by the lack of cooperation and arrogance of Peppino Saconne. One of them had referred to him as a creepy bastard who seemed to be one step away from totally losing it. Volatile, like a bubbling volcano about to blow.

They had also noticed that he seemed to have a disturbing effect on his staff, especially the females, who made a deliberate attempt to keep out of his way, almost cringing if they were unfortunate enough to attract his attention.

Don Saconne finished the call with relief. He hoped he had sounded normal. He didn't mention the fury he felt after a visit from the stupid fat idiot, Peppino kept around to do his dirty work. Accompanied by an equally brainless sidekick, Gianni had sauntered into the house as if he owned it. No manners, so rude and arrogant, he'd handed over an envelope with an air of self- importance, then had the audacity to stand there expecting some remuneration for delivering it. Don Saconne had pointedly turned and walked out of the reception area saying as he went, 'See yourselves out.'

He took a deep breath as he opened the envelope. Where on earth did Peppino find those people?

Inside was a legal document related to the lading of a shipment of second hand farm machinery from Russia which was now sitting on the Palermo docks waiting for collection. As he read on further he saw that Peppino had added another person's name to both of theirs as a new partner. A name that made his blood run cold. A man from across the sea, from Libya, someone he vowed he would never do business with again. Don Saconne had given some tough orders over the years, some of which he occasionally had doubts about, although he could always justify making them, but, he sometimes felt that when he finally left this world, he might have some explaining to do...What this man and his associates had done was something he could not condone and felt uneasy profiting from it.

Peppino had been behind the whole thing. He had introduced them and set up the partnership. Don Saconne regretted not having taken a more active role in checking out what was involved. Against his better judgement he had put Peppino in charge, in preparation for when he took over leadership of the family. What had happened was diabolical, and even now as he thought about it, he clasped the crucifix he wore around his neck, and prayed.

A shipment of young people and children, who had come from goodness knows where, had been brought in as human commodities, part of the lucrative trade in harvested body organs. It was against everything he believed in, and he was still haunted by their faces. Under Peppino's orders, they had been taken to the family beach house in Santa Flavia, where a deregistered doctor had set up a primitive, makeshift surgery which was supposed to provide organs for a waiting list of mainly wealthy, ill, old people. When Don Saconne realised what this business deal had involved, it appalled him so much, that one night, from his office, he made an anonymous phone call to the Questura. There was a subsequent raid, led by Commissario Lombardo, and the children had been rescued in time. A lot of money had been lost, and many disappointed people didn't get their promised organs, but Don Saconne felt better. He knew Peppino owed the man from Libya a lot of money, and he believed this new partnership had something to do with the repayment of it.

It was true, the innocent shipment of farm machinery was not as it seemed. Hidden in spare parts, welded into the crevices of the metal were packets of uncut heroin that would, after several stop-offs, make their way into the markets of Sicily and Southern Italy. It was Peppino's business deal, the don's name was there as a formality, and the Libyan's name had been added as payment for what was owed to him.

He put the envelope on his desk, then tried to forget about it for the moment. He knew sooner or later Peppino would be in touch. All he could do was wait and hope that not too much damage had been done.

After saying goodbye to Don Saconne, Lombardo decided to go down to the docks and see what was going on. If the Saconne family had a shipment coming in, that meant Peppino would be in the area, checking on its progress. He wished he had known that before, when they had found Doni's body. He was also worried about Jonno and wondered if anyone had heard anything yet. He would call in on Rose after he had finished looking for Peppino. There was no doubt in his mind that by now she would have heard about Doni and that would have made her even more anxious.

It was busy at the docks, and as he walked down row after row of containers sitting waiting for collection, he realised how hopeless the whole thing was. He needed twenty officers, not just one, if his search was to succeed. A few people who knew him called out greetings, others stood and stared, wondering what had brought him down here again.

'Seen Peppino Saconne lately?' He asked a man driving a forklift.

'Yes, he was here this afternoon, further down, near that office, talking to some guy. He looked pretty angry, doing a lot of shouting, then he stormed off to the car park and drove away. What a crazy one,' and he made circles with his finger at the side of his head. 'I'd hate to get in his bad books.'

He then started up the engine and drove off.

That's interesting, I wonder what caused him to become so upset? Lombardo thought, as he left the harbour area.

Walking down towards Rose's salon, he suddenly realised that it was Saturday night, the days seemed to have got away from him. Had it really been almost a week since he had been in Taormina? It seemed far longer, and despite his best efforts, he had made no headway in getting to the bottom of any of these mysteries. Doni was dead, Jonno.... who knows what had happened to him, and Angela, where on earth was she? He kept coming back to Peppino Saconne. I'm sure he's involved somehow. I just hope she's alright. I still can't work out why they have her and why no contact has been made. These thoughts kept him busy until he looked up and saw the salon was just around the corner.

As he got closer, he heard loud wails coming from inside, quickening his step he looked inside and found a group of women, plus several boys sitting around a distraught Rose who was holding a small box in her hand.

Lombardo went over to her, talking soothingly until he could see what was in the box. 'Calm down Rose, what has happened?' He looked closely at the contents. It was a bloody ear. An earring still attached to it.

'It's Jonno's!' Rose cried. 'It's his, that's his earring, I gave it to him.'

Patting her shoulder gently, he asked, 'when did you get it? Who delivered it?'

One of the boys answered. 'Someone on a bike rode by, and gave it to the receptionist. It had Rose's name written on it, so she opened it, and saw this. There was a message too.' 'Last chance. More body parts will be delivered unless you pay back the money.'

'What money? Do you know anything about this?'

The boy answered. 'All I know is that Jonno said he had a job in Catania. He was going with Doni. They left a few days ago, Wednesday I think.'

'But Doni's body was found on Thursday night,' Lombardo said. He certainly didn't go to Catania and I don't think Jonno made it there either. I'm sure it was a ploy to get them away from their friends so that they were on their own and vulnerable. What on earth could they have got themselves involved in?

What money is he supposed to have taken? It must have made someone very angry.

Does anyone have any idea if he's been doing business in the Mercato lately, stepping on someone's toes, taking something that's not his, helping himself to it.... What a silly young fool!

I wonder if it could have anything to do with what happened earlier, that fight between the La Kalsa and Albergheria boys? Do either of you know anything about this?'

He looked closely at the two boys. 'Have either of you heard of Il Gattopardo?'

They stared back at him, their faces expressionless.

Chapter 16

Angela lay crying on the bed. Maria looked at her, pity in her eyes.

'You know I can't do anything, I'm sorry, if I could I would help, but what they would do to me if they found out, I can't, I just can't. I'm sorry, really, really sorry,' and she left the room, locking the door after her.

Angela must have fallen asleep, for when she opened her eyes it seemed that it was now late afternoon. The house was quiet except for the sound of the sea; it's waves crashing against the cliffs nearby. Her sadness had now been replaced by a strong determination to get off the island, but working out how to do it was the problem facing her now.

Suddenly, she heard voices coming from below, talking to Maria. It sounded like Aurelio and also, as another voice spoke, Susan. What were they doing here, maybe looking for her? She tried to shout out and bang on the door, but all she could hear was Maria's voice telling them that no one was home and maybe come back another time, or even better still, ring the master and speak to him, rather than making another wasted journey back here. Then, she heard Aurelio telling Maria they were going to spend the night on the island as Signora Susan wanted to take a tour the next day and explore the whole place.

They would come back then and speak to Mr. Peppino if he was home.

Angela could hear their voices as they climbed back into the car. The sound of them leaving made her burst into tears again and she threw herself back onto the bed. After she calmed down she began to think of ways she could get their attention and let them know where she was. All she knew was that Peppino wanted her father's co-operation and he was using her safety as a bargaining tool. She had all night to think and plan some sort of strategy. She was determined that when they came back she would find a way to let them know that she was here in this villa, being held in a room right above them.

Susan and Aurelio were enjoying a well-deserved dinner after the long and tiring day. Although they had little to show for their efforts they felt that all had not been wasted. Sooner or later Peppino would come back to Levanzo and they would ask him the questions they wanted answers to. They had plenty of time to wait. The more Aurelio thought about it the more he thought his cousin was behind much of what was going on. Why? Was what he didn't know. After leaving the villa they had booked into a small family run bed and breakfast. It was owned by friends of Aurelio's father. They were staunch supporters of his charities, and committed to employing refugees in a variety of jobs. One of their great success stories was a young woman, who had spent several years in refugee camps before arriving in Porto Empedocle. She had trained as a chef and was now featured regularly on cooking shows. People came from far and wide to enjoy the food. Her dishes were considered unique, largely influenced by Sicilian and North African traditions.

The setting was beautiful, a small trattoria by the sheltered harbour. Stars were beginning to come out in the clear summer night sky and a gentle wind cooled the heat from a day that was almost at its end. Sitting in the tranquil setting, it was easy to forget for a moment the trouble and uncertainty around them. Aurelio kept talking about Angela, how strong and capable she was, resourceful too. It was as if by talking, he was also convincing himself that they would find her and everything would be fine. Susan kept reassuring him with supportive words as well as trying to distract him by asking him questions about his university course.

'I'm interested in the events which happened in Palermo in the nineteen nineties,' he replied, after Susan had asked him why he was studying that particular degree.

'You know that Commissario Lombardo's uncle was killed in an ambush during that time? He was part of a detail protecting a well-known judge. When my father talks about it, which is not often, there is still a sense of anger and shock. Because they chose to fight against the evil influences infecting the poor and helpless, many good men and women lost their lives. 'They died for what they believed in, trying to make things right.

It is still problematic for my father of course, because his brother, Don Saconne, was involved in some way, although there is no real proof. The police and other authorities have tried for years to link him to those events, as well as a few others, but for some reason the people who could have given evidence disappeared.

He was able to get away scott free and the terrible thing is that he continues his life as if he's blameless. When I finish this degree, I will study law and then hopefully get a job with the Guardia di Finanza. I am fascinated by crimes involving money and money trails.'

They had just finished their primo secondo of grilled swordfish and roasted vegetables, when a low-slung sports car roared past them up the winding road, disappearing around the bend in the direction of Peppino's house.

'I bet that's him, at least we know he'll be at home tomorrow morning. I don't think it would solve anything by going up there tonight. If we have a good night's sleep we will be able to handle it better, don't you think?' Aurelio looked at Susan.

She nodded in agreement. 'Yes, definitely, I think going up to the house tomorrow is a much better idea. I'm sure nothing is going to change between now and then.'

The roar of a car driving up to the house woke Angela from an uneasy nap. She had finally fallen asleep after exhausting herself trying to think of a plan which would alert Aurelio to where she was. She sat up and listened. The door downstairs opened and she could hear voices, they sounded loud and over excited. She recognised Aurelio's as being the loudest. As far as it was possible for her to understand, as she could only hear parts of the conversation, he was talking about a meeting he had come from and how happy he had been with the result. They moved off into another room and their voices faded away.

Maria had been up earlier with a tray. Angela had not realised how hungry she was and ate the delicious meal of lasagne and salad. She also enjoyed the bottle of wine which had accompanied it. The food and wine had calmed her and she now felt able to cope with her situation. She suddenly heard footsteps coming up the stairs and the door to her room opened. Peppino stood in the doorway, a sneering look on his cruel face.

'I hear we had some visitors today?'

He looked at her intently, but she remained expressionless and didn't answer. I'm not letting him know a thing. Angela thought to herself. She stared back at him in silence. 'Now that Aurelio has come looking for you, I'll have to put those plans I mentioned to you in motion sooner than I wanted to, but anyway we can't help that....'

'I'm ringing your father tonight and putting a proposition to him. If he agrees, all will be well, but if he refuses, then we will have to rethink our plans.

It won't be good for you or your family if he refuses and sadly for you it will show what little value he places on your life.'

He attempted to smile at her, his thin mouth curving on either side of his hollow cheeks. Peppino was someone for whom smiling was not a natural expression and Angela found it slightly unnerving looking at him trying.

'I'll put the business proposal to him, if he accepts, you will be released tomorrow, if not, we may have to resort to offering him some inducements to help him make the right choice. I'll speak to you again after I've finished speaking to him and let you know how things went. By the way, is Maria looking after you? You have plenty of food? Ok, fingers crossed that your father sees sense and agrees.'

He left the room, the sound of the lock turning over with a final click. Angela was left alone again feeling puzzled and slightly afraid. She knew her father would not be willing to let Peppino anywhere near his bank under normal circumstances, but this was not normal.

Peppino Saconne stood waiting, the phone to his ear, listening as the ring tone droned on and on. Eventually, it was answered and he recognised the voice of Angela's father Rocco Salvino. 'Pronto.'

'Good evening sir, sorry to bother you at this late hour, but this is quite urgent, at least I think you'll agree that it is when I put this proposal to you. I don't want to put pressure on you but I do need an answer quickly......... say in the next day or two.

To help you make the right decision, and at the same time realise the urgency, I wanted to let you know that Angela is here with me.

I've been lucky to have had the pleasure of your daughter's company over the last few days and will continue to have her here until we can come to a suitable arrangement. She is a lovely girl and we are doing our best to make her stay comfortable while she is here with us.'

A lengthy silence followed, finally broken when Rocco Salvino answered.

'She's with you, Peppino? I have to tell you; we've already filed a missing person report. The police are looking for her, and here you are telling me she is with you?

Why, for goodness sake? What on earth is she doing with you? Why has it taken you so long to contact me? We've been worried sick, the whole family has......'

'I've already told you why. I have a business proposition for you, and she is here with me as …. if you like… some insurance, so that you will happily agree with the proposal I am about to put to you.

The thing is I have a large sum of money that I need to put in a safe bank and at the same time invest in some government tenders, which, I happen to know, you have a real chance of getting. In particular, the one for the extension of the shipping yards at the docks in Palermo. That would be of great benefit to my import/export business,' and he finished with a laugh.

'I can't just agree to that over the phone. I have to look at the proposal first. You are aware that I have board members with whom I have to consult before I can approve something. I don't operate alone, Peppino, and on top of that, you don't have the best reputation. The word is, that people are wary of doing any business with you. Your track record doesn't inspire much confidence.

Those shady deals that have been investigated by several police forces both here in Sicily, and further afield. I heard whispers recently, that the Guardia di Finanza was looking very closely at one of your business associates, someone from Libya.'

There was a silence, and when Peppino chose to speak again, his voice had changed. No longer sounding pleasant and business like, it was now low and menacing.

'The thing is Salvino, do you want to see your daughter again? If you don't agree, I'm sorry, but the chances of your daughter returning home to the comfort of her loving family are almost nil and there will most likely be a very sad outcome. It's up to you. Agree, and she's back with you tomorrow.'

'I can't believe what you are saying. Do you really think you can get away with this? What you are doing is criminal!' Rocco Salvino's voice broke with emotion.

Peppino continued in an expressionless tone. 'Well, sir, I hope that I'll have your answer tomorrow by four pm., that should give you plenty of time to speak to your board members and put forward a convincing reason as to why you have agreed to accept my money. If I haven't heard from you by then, your daughter will be delivered to you in a condition that will be incredibly traumatic for you and your family.

Another thing, don't mention this phone call to anyone and certainly not the police, otherwise, things will become worse, both for you, and your daughter,' and with that, he hung up.

Smiling to himself, he walked back upstairs. It was a bit of a bother having Angela up there. I should have taken her to Santa Flavia, he reflected.... The journey from Palermo and the ferry crossing was becoming tiresome. Never mind, it won't be for much longer.

He decided to give her a nightcap which should keep her quiet until tomorrow. Then he would reassess the situation. Hopefully, the decision that Salvino made would be the one he wanted. It was such a nuisance getting rid of bodies and he hoped he wouldn't have to tomorrow.

The syringe in his pocket was filled with a sample of the product from his most recent business venture. This would be a good trial run. He hoped it would be successful.

The next morning, after finishing breakfast, Susan and Aurelio set off for Peppino's house. They knew he was there and they were determined to confront him with their suspicions.

As they drew up outside the house, they saw his car was still there. That was good, he hadn't suddenly taken off during the night. Aurelio rang the bell and a few minutes later the door was opened by Maria. Her hair was tied up in a scarf and she had a duster in her hand. She gave no sign that she recognised them from their previous visit.' Yes, can I help you?'

'Good morning, remember me? I'm Aurelio, Peppino's cousin. I called in yesterday but Peppino wasn't around. We decided to stay over for a few more days, I'm showing my friend the sights. I saw his car parked outside, so I'm pretty sure he's at home now. It's been a while since we last caught up and seeing as I'm on the island, I just wanted call in and say hi.' He smiled at her, but received nothing in return.

'I'll just go and check.'

She turned her back on them and disappeared into the house, it was at least fifteen minutes before anyone came. Peppino finally appeared wearing a pair of swimming trunks, a towel slung around his shoulders.

'Hi coz,' he grabbed Aurelio in a bear hug and squeezed him hard. 'It's been a long time, too long. How are you? Come in. Who's your friend?'

Aurelio made the introductions as they walked through the house and then out on to the terrace. A large pool lay ahead of them. Several sun lounges and umbrellas were dotted around it, and at its edge, the blue outline of the Mediterranean Sea, sparkling in the sun.

'Well it's great to see you, coz. Would you like a coffee or something else, juice, water?' They both asked for a coffee, and while they were waiting, Aurelio brought up the subject of Don Saconne.

I saw your dad, yesterday he was looking well. We called in because we thought you might have been there. My friend Angela is missing; you remember her don't you? Rocco Salvino's daughter. I brought her here, to one of your parties.'

'Yeah, yeah, I remember. Pretty little thing. What makes you think I'd be interested in the fact that she's missing? As a matter of fact, I've been in Palermo for the last couple of days, sorting out some business.' There was a slight smirk on his face as he answered.

'No problem, I'm just asking around. Thought you might have heard something.'

'Well, I haven't!' He answered vehemently. Both Aurelio and Susan couldn't help but notice a slight shifting of his eyes over to the house, in particular a window with blue shutters that were firmly shut.

The conversation suddenly shifted when Peppino asked Susan what were her favourite places in Sicily, following on with a few superficial questions about her life in Australia. He was obviously in a hurry to get rid of them and was desperately looking for an excuse.

'I have to drive back to Palermo soon,' he said, picking up his phone. 'It was nice to see you again Aurelio, don't wait so long next time ok? Good to meet you too, Signora Susan, enjoy the rest of your holiday in Sicily.'

They had no choice but to follow him back into the house and he quickly escorted them out the door, watching as they drove off.

'He's lying!' Susan looked at Aurelio as they drove away from the house. 'He's lying!' She repeated 'I know he is. Don't you agree? Did you see his sneaky look, over towards the house? He's either taken her and is keeping her here, for whatever reason, or he knows where she is. Don't you agree Aurelio?'

'There is definitely something fishy going on there. I just can't work out what it is. I think we should stay here for a few more days. Do you have any plans for the next couple of days Susan?'

'No, I don't, and I think you are right. We should keep an eye on the house and see who comes and goes. I hate the thought of leaving here without knowing if she's there or not. I would never forgive myself if something happened to her and we were here all the time.'

'When we get back to the B&B I'll give her father a ring. I have met him at different functions and he is a good man, despite being such a successful, high profile businessman. He has helped my father a few times with donations to his charities and finding employment for refugees.'

'We could also contact Commissario Lombardo, he might have heard something too,' Susan added, a little hopefully.

As soon as they got back to the B&B Aurelio called Rocco Salvino. He answered almost immediately, it was as if he had been expecting a call.

'Good afternoon sir, it's Aurelio, Aurelio Saconne, Angela's friend.'

There was a short silence, followed by a sharp intake of breath and then Rocco Salvino spoke. 'Hello Aurelio, how are you?'

'I'm fine sir, I was just wondering if there was any news about Angela.? I've been so worried about her, have the police found out anything yet? Is there anything I can do to help?'

The words rushed out and he barely drew breath. 'Sorry, sorry sir, I don't want to upset you, I just wondered...' He suddenly stopped and tears filled his eyes. Susan put a hand on his shoulder and tried to calm him.

Rocco Salvino's voice came back and filled the emptiness.

'No, no I haven't, Aurelio. The police are doing their best, but it's as if she has vanished into thin air.'

'You haven't received any messages, sir? I've been racking my brains trying to think of a reason why she has disappeared.'

'No, Aurelio, I haven't a clue.'

'Are you sure sir, just the smallest idea, even if you think it's silly or far-fetched?'

'No, I can't think of anything, it's best if we leave it to the police, they know what they're doing. It's probably a case of mistaken identity or a not very funny prank. We should just wait for a few more days, I'm sure the police will find her.'

Rocco Salvino sounded so unconvincing as he attempted to make out that all was well. It was as if he knew something and was trying his damnedest to pretend he didn't, while at the same time allaying their fears.

Aurelio promised not do anything until he had spoken to him again, and he finished the call feeling that he had accomplished very little. The only thing he was sure of was that Rocco Salvino was lying, just like Peppino Saconne.

'That was a waste of time, except I'm sure he knows something about Angela's disappearance. I'm not giving up. We just have to keep watching the house and hope that Peppino slips up, and when he does, then we'll go in and find out what is going on.' Susan nodded in agreement, yes all they could do was watch and wait.

Poor, poor Angela. Susan hoped she was alright, and as she sat there, looking at those steep jagged white cliffs with the sea crashing far below, she said a silent prayer. Please keep Angela safe.

Chapter 17

Commissario Lombardo left Rose's salon, after promising that he would try and find out what had happened to Jonno. He had packed up the severed ear and was now on his way to the Forensic Laboratory where hopefully some answers might be found, such as what sort of knife was used, and where the crime had taken place. Looking at recent events, he didn't hold out much hope for Jonno, but at the same time he was trying to keep optimistic. Jonno was a reckless young man but he didn't deserve this.

He had almost reached the Questura when his phone rang. It was his uncle.

'Luca, can you call in at the refuge when you have a moment, we've got a bit of a problem here?' His voice sounded calm, but knowing his uncle, that wasn't necessarily a true indication of how he was feeling.

'I'm close by, I'll be about twenty minutes. I just have to drop something off at the office.'

After leaving the ear at the lab with instructions to check it as quickly as possible, Lombardo reached the refuge in good time. It was quiet so the children were probably at school, only the father and two women were there. As he reached the door, his uncle quickly took him into a room at the back, which

Lombardo knew was set up as a small clinic. Lying on a bed in the corner, with a bandage covering half his face, was Jonno. He looked very unwell and as the two men came up to the bed he looked up at the priest and Lombardo, his face racked with pain.

'What happened Jonno? I've just come from your sister and she gave me an ear, obviously yours.' He stared at the bloody bandage. 'Who did this to you?'

He then turned to the priest, 'How did he get here? The ear was delivered to his sister with a threat.'

'What have you done Jonno?' he turned to him.

'He literally crawled in here about thirty minutes ago, hysterical and raving about escaping from a building, after being abducted off a bus.'

'Yes, we have a witness who was on that bus and reported the abduction. We've had a watch out for him ever since.'

'What I'd like to know, Jonno, is what you have done to piss off someone so badly, that they shot, then dumped your friend Doni's body down at the docks and cut your ear off. Your sister told me you'd got a job in Catania, and now here you are, minus an ear and your friend dead. So that job obviously didn't work out, if there ever was one at all!

Come on! You've got some explaining to do.' Lombardo stared down at him, a look of frustration on his face.

'It's a long story,' Jonno stared up at him,

'Well I've got plenty of time.'

And in a weak, fretful voice Jonno proceeded to tell his story...

He and his gang had been given a prime dealing spot in the Mercato di Ballaro` and there, they kept an uneasy truce with another gang, who also worked a section nearby. The people who controlled the business worked for the Saconne family. They did the drops and collected the money at the end of each day. The gangs divided what was left after a hefty cut had been taken. It was also those people who had the last say in who got what and where they were allowed to sell it. Jonno continued, one of the bosses said that they needed he and Doni to go and take care of something near Catania. Some people hadn't done the right thing, a deal had gone wrong, and he and Doni had been given the chance to prove themselves by fixing the problem. If they did it to the boss's satisfaction, they could possibly move up the ladder and be given more responsibility.... a leadership role, they said. Because they didn't have any travelling money and were too scared to ask for any, they kept back some of the takings from the day's dealing and also kept a bit of the unsold product as a backup in case they needed more. It wasn't much, two hundred euros and two small bags. When they returned, they would pay it back after they were paid for doing the job.

Only it hadn't worked out that way. After they arrived at a house somewhere near Catania it had become obvious that what they had walked into was trouble. The word was, a boat full of refugees had been massacred. Who had done it was still a mystery, but it had cost the organisers an enormous amount of money. It had been a failed investment. There would be no profits to fund new activities, in fact some of the investors now owed money. Things were not looking good. It was Doni's and Jonno's job to be go betweens between the disgruntled parties. Because they were Nigerian their employers hoped it would be seen as a gesture of goodwill and help ease the tensions which had arisen after the loss of the merchandise and money.

Lombardo listened to this strange story intently.

'Well, what happened? Who were those groups, and did you recognise anyone?'

Jonno stared up at him, gave a long sigh, and continued.

'I knew one of them, he's connected to the Saconne's. I'd seen a couple of the others around, you know, at a club and down at the market, not to talk to, but I knew who they were. Some Nigerians, a few Libyans.......'

The group sounded to Lombardo like the usual mixture of newcomers plus some disgruntled former members of gangs from outside, who had formed an uneasy alliance and were now starting to make a name for themselves around town. They were obviously getting noticed by their rivals.

Jonno gave a rueful smile. 'It was that group who told us to go down there. Things were going ok, we seemed to be helping but it was hard to know, and looking back now, I don't think it was ever meant to work. It was a set up and we were stuck in the middle. Expendable. Then things suddenly changed a couple of nights ago. Someone new came to the house, someone who's presence changed everything. Doni disappeared. People knew about us taking the money and drugs. They wanted to use us as examples so others wouldn't try the same thing.

It was just an excuse to create a huge amount of trouble, to get the rivals heated up. Normally they are ok with a bit of borrowing as long as it's paid back, but this was a deliberate move to make trouble.

I never saw Doni again. He was my brother; he didn't want any trouble.'

'So you know what happened to him then?' Lombardo asked.

'I had a bad feeling, and then, when they took me off the bus the other day....' His voice choked. 'I was just trying to get back here, and hide out for a while. As soon as they took Doni away I knew things were bad, so I left, snuck off ...... I had to get away, anywhere. I knew staying there wasn't safe. After they took me off the bus, they told me then. 'Do you want to end up like your friend, a bullet to the head and then dumped in with the fishes? Just pay the money back, give back what you took and we'll go easy on you.' That's what they said. I knew they were trying to frighten me, that was obvious. I also didn't believe they would go easy on me. They had to have been following the bus. Someone must have given me away. I didn't think anyone saw me, I did my best to stay out of sight. I was so sure nobody saw me leave the house. They took me to a place, some sort of hideout I think. They beat me up a bit. I told them I didn't have the money, that Doni had it and the drugs too. They didn't believe me. Then this animal, a bloody animal got a knife and cut off my ear!'

He felt the bandage, covering where his ear had been, and the tears came faster. 'I didn't have what they wanted,' he kept repeating.

Father Benedict patted him gently on his shoulder. 'It's ok Jonno, you're safe now. Someone could have recognised you on the bus, all they had to do was make a phone call. I suppose we'll never know. Those families have such a stranglehold over people, you don't know who to trust.'

'They used me to send a message to the others, I know. Stirring up trouble. The Saconne's want a war. They sent my ear to my sister… as if she could repay them. My poor sister, she must be so worried.'

'I've seen her,' Lombardo said. 'She gave me your ear; it's being tested in the lab. When the results come back I don't think there will be any surprises. I'll message her now and tell her you're safe.

I also want to know how you managed to escape? It sounds as if they had you locked away pretty securely.'

'I was lucky, real lucky. After they cut my ear, the pain was terrible. One of them went out with the ear, so only one was left. I was screaming really loudly, then I pretended to be unconscious. The guy ran out of the room, to get some water or something and didn't lock the door. As soon as he left I got up and climbed out a back window, then ran and ran until I found a road that led down to the sea. I knew if I followed the shoreline I would eventually get to an area I knew, so I walked and walked, resting now and then when I thought it was safe. When it was dark, I was able to get close to Father Benedict's centre. I stayed in a small storage unit nearby. I must have fallen asleep for a few hours; I was pretty exhausted. Then when I woke up I came straight here.'

'I'm glad you got away Jonno, if you hadn't, you probably would have ended up like your friend. I think now might be a good time to reassess your future. When you are feeling a bit better we'll have another talk about what we can do to keep you safe.

You certainly aren't here. You can stay with Father Benedict for a few days at most. But once word gets out, and believe me it will, they will come looking for you. We both know they don't like unfinished business, especially if they feel they have lost out.'

'I have a friend, a priest, from an order of monks who live in a monastery high in the Hyblaean mountains. I think it would be best if I send you there tomorrow, Jonno. I just have to speak to him and then work out how to get you there.'

Father Benedict took out his phone. 'I'll have to keep you away from the children too. They get over excited and might spill the beans accidently. You know how they love secrets, but are so bad at keeping them.' He smiled and left the room to make the call.

'It's time to try and have a chat with Peppino Saconne again. I have been looking for him but he always seems to be a few steps ahead. It's as if he doesn't want me to find him.'

'I don't know if it's helpful but there was a name I heard a few times, I just know that when that name was mentioned people looked uneasy and even frightened.' Jonno added, as the commissario was leaving. 'Il Gattopardo. Have you heard that name before sir?' Lombardo stopped in his tracks, turning, he replied, 'yes, yes I have.' Then he walked out the door.

There was that name again! Il Gattopardo, the Leopard. The name that Stefano said made the boys in the lockup turn pale and become silent.

'Anyone seen Peppino Saconne?' Lombardo inquired, as he walked into the Questura. A few officers were standing around at the reception desk and looked at him expectantly. 'What's he done now?' One of them asked.

'I think he's behind the murder down at the docks. We might have the beginning of a gang war on our hands, and his name keeps coming up time and time again. I want to nip it in the bud before it gets the chance to take off. I don't want a return of the eighties and nineties. Have a word to your 'canaries' out there and let me know if anything comes up.'

He continued on his way up the stairs. The men below disbursed and went off to see which of their informers was willing to sing.

Chapter 18

The door opened and Peppino walked in, a deeply satisfied look on his face. Angela got up from the bed where she had been lying, ever since Peppino had left to phone her father.

'Have you spoken to my father?' She asked, almost afraid to hear his answer.

'Yes, but he's taking a bit of time to give me an answer. I thought given the circumstances, he would have said yes straightaway.

You'd better hope that by this time tomorrow, he has made the right choice.' Peppino answered callously. 'Meanwhile, I've got something that will help you get through the next twenty-four hours, I don't want you lying here feeling anxious,' and he pulled the syringe out of his pocket. His strong arms pushed her back down on the bed, and before she could fight back, he pushed the needle into her arm. Almost immediately she felt a wave of lightheadedness sweep over her and she fell into a deep sleep.

He carefully locked the door and went back downstairs. 'Come on let's go,' he said to Gianni. 'I have to go back to Palermo, something important has come up and I have to deal with it straight away.'

'Maria, we're leaving now. I don't think I'll be back until tomorrow. Our guest is sleeping at the moment, just keep an eye on her and let me know if I have any more visitors, or if anything happens I should know about.' And with that they left the house, speeding down the winding road that led to the ferry and on to Palermo.

When Lombardo came back to his office, there were two messages on his desk. One was from Rocco Salvino, the other from an acquaintance in the Maltese Maritime Squadron. He had met Matteo Vella several years ago at a joint Sicilian/ Maltese training exercise, the aim of which was to look at strategies to deal with the boatloads of refugees coming across the Mediterranean Sea from Libya and through into Italy. It hadn't achieved much in the end, but Lombardo and Vella had recognised they had similar problems dealing with their respective bureaucracies and agreed to work together if the need arose, bypassing the red tape of their own countries. It was common knowledge that Malta and Libya had some sort of agreement wherein the authorities in Malta would let the Libyans know if boats were sighted in the waters near their island. They would then come and take them back to where they had set sail from. Many believed this was not the best outcome.

The message from Vella was to let him know they had received some intelligence that a boat was on its way to Sicily. For some unknown reason it had been allowed through without the usual interception. This was not normal, which led him to believe that perhaps, people with important connections were involved. He thought Lombardo might like to check it out at his end. This was very interesting, especially in light of what had happened recently. He would get on to the Sicilian Coast Guard to see if they could track it and keep him updated.

He then turned his attention to the message from Rocco Salvino.

I wonder if he's had any news about Angela? he thought, as he rang Salvino's number. He answered straight away, and wasted no time getting to the point, giving Lombardo the details of the phone call from Peppino Saconne.

He told the commissario about the veiled threats, the attempt at blackmail and the idea that his bank would damage its excellent reputation to become a money laundering front for the tainted profits of that family.

He continued on, emotionally describing how Peppino had threatened to cause harm to Angela if he didn't agree to his demands. It was ridiculous. At first he had been frightened for his daughter's safety but the more he thought about it the more he wanted to confront that foolish, delusional person, and let him know his threats meant nothing. He wanted to know if the commissario agreed with what he had said and if he could help him. Maybe by bringing in Peppino Saconne and holding him until they had found Angela. 'Don't you agree, Commissario?' Lombardo thought for a moment, this seemed a little reckless, like waving a red flag in front of a bull, but on the other hand he could understand Salvino's frustration and anger. This was a banker who guarded his reputation fiercely and wasn't going to throw it away because of some threats from a criminal with a reputation for instability.

'Well, sir, I agree that you definitely shouldn't give in to his demands, but can you wait a little before you tell him. The longer you are able to stall him the more chance we have of finding him. Most importantly, whatever you do don't let him know you have no intention of going along with his demands. That would really set him off.

Let me try and bring him in first, if we can find him. He's not been seen for a couple of days and we are trying our best to track him down. I have officers out looking now, but so far we have come up with nothing. Did he give you any clue as to where he was holding her or where he was ringing from? That would be helpful.'

'No, not a thing, sorry.'

'Well just sit tight, don't ring him. My officers and I will keep looking and let you know immediately, if we have any news. Try to stay calm, and most of all don't let anyone else know. I don't want the press getting hold of this and putting it out there. If he finds out that you have contacted the police things could become very dangerous for your daughter.' Lombardo finished the call and went back downstairs.

The desk sergeant, put down the phone and called out to the commissario as he came down the stairs. 'We've had a sighting sir.' He was on the ferry coming from Levanzo, someone recognised him and his sidekick. I'd say they're either going to the father's house in Terrasini or on to Palermo.'

'I think he will be coming here to Palermo,' Lombardo said. 'He has a lot of problems that need dealing with straight away, so it makes sense that he should come here. He has an apartment near the docks doesn't he? Ok. We'll put a car near the father's house, just in case he calls in there, and I want a couple of cars stationed near that apartment.

I want to know the moment he appears. We need to bring him in, or at the least, follow his movements. I'm worried about Angela Salvino; I don't want him harming her. I need to know where he is at all times. Don't let him get away. He's a slippery one, and we can't afford to lose him. I don't want him anywhere near Father Benedict's refuge either. Hopefully they will have moved Jonno to a safe place by now, but we can't take any chances.

Let me have two officers, Rizzo and Marino will do.'

He walked out the door and met the two officers outside.

'We'll go to the apartment first and find a spot to park out of the way where he won't see us.'

The apartment looked deserted. The shutters were closed and the huge front door was shut and locked. A big iron bolt firmly in place. Lombardo and his men sat in the car for two hours watching for signs of life, but no one went in or out. Surprisingly, they reached the frustrating conclusion that Peppino was not coming to the apartment.

He checked with the officers who were keeping watch on the house in Terrasini. He hadn't been there either. Where on earth was he? Lombardo racked his brain trying to think of another place he might head to. The house in Santa Flavia, that was worth a try. It was a while since he had been there and now, as he thought about it, he felt sick to his stomach, remembering the poor children they had rescued from the human traffickers last year. Yes, that was definitely a possibility. In fact, the more he thought about it the more sense it made. It wouldn't surprise him if that was where they had taken Jonno after they had abducted him from the bus. It was worth a look at anyway.

'We'll go and check out the house in Santa Flavia,' he instructed his men, and they headed off down to the seaside village.

They had made good time and turned off the busy main road only forty minutes after leaving Palermo. Luckily the traffic was light. People were probably soaking up the sun, enjoying their summer holiday. The narrow bumpy track they had turned into, led them down towards the sea. Tangled bushes lay in dry clumps in the dusty earth. As they drove on they noticed an eerie silence, broken only by the sound of their tyres crunching over the stones. Up ahead were huge metal gates. Lombardo wondered if he would have to use the bolt cutters he always kept in the boot, along with an assortment of other tools. You never knew what might come in handy.

Surprisingly they weren't locked. After one of his men opened them, they drove on through, leaving them open in case they needed back up or to beat a hasty retreat. Better to be prepared, he thought. Finally they reached the beach house. It was a rambling, stone building with spacious verandas and a neglected garden. It was probably used only once or twice a year, even less now that there were no family members around who would want to. Recently, it had been used for a very different purpose, a far more sinister one.

They pulled up and got out, their handguns at the ready. Who knew what sort of welcome they might receive. It was still silent. No one came out. There must be someone there, a low slung sports car was parked around the corner of the house, but the wide verandahs were empty. The three men crept slowly in a single file up to what looked like the main entrance, their weapons out.

It seemed almost surreal, except the last time Lombardo had been here, it was a pitch black night. The only light had come from their torches and the stars. They had found the children huddled in an outhouse guarded by heavily armed thugs. It was a short bloody battle, several of the hoodlums had been killed, but thankfully all of the children were saved, and only two of his men had suffered superficial wounds. Now, here he was again, only this time in daylight, and it certainly didn't look as sinister.

The house was empty. Each room they went into showed no sign that anyone had been there for quite a while. No smell of cigarettes or food. A light dust covered everything. 'Nothing here boss,' one of the officers called out from another room.

'Let's take a walk down towards the sea, I know there are several outbuildings and a boat house at the bottom of the property. Just keep your eyes open, that parked car tells me that someone is definitely around, so don't let your guard down for a minute.'

They headed down towards the shoreline, looking left and right, until they came to a building that had the appearance it was used for storage. Cautiously pushing open the door, they walked into an empty room. There was a difference though. Scratched into the mud rendered walls were names. There were pleas for help. Some were just a name, others, messages for loved ones which would never be read by them. The voices of people who had been victims of people trafficking over the years. The men stood there, unable to speak, reading those names and messages. On the ground were chains and other sorts of restraints which had been used to keep the victims' prisoner.

'We'll need to record all of this,' Lombardo said. 'Those names need to be traced. I'll get in touch with some people from the refugee task force. I can't let those people remain anonymous. We owe it to them and their families to at least try.

Let's continue down, and see what other surprises are waiting for us.'

The men reached another building, but this time they looked beyond it down to the beach. There was a small jetty, where a yellow wooden boat was tied up, rocking gently in the waves.

A man's body lay on the sand near the water. As they got closer they could see that he was face down and at the back of his head was a bullet hole. There was not a lot of blood, and if you couldn't see the wound, you might have thought he was having a nap. His shirt and pants were clean and fresh looking and he was still wearing a pair of sandals.

Lombardo looked down and gently turned him over. Peppino Saconne stared up at him, the cruel mouth locked into a sneer. The three officers stood speechless. Their investigation had suddenly taken a dramatic turn. Lombardo took out his phone and started to make the first of several calls.

Chapter 19

After they had seen Peppino Saconne's car drive away, Susan and Aurelio decided to go back to the house and see if they could find any evidence of Angela's presence. 'I'm sure that maid knows something,' Susan said.

'Yes, I think so too,' Aurelio agreed, leading the way up to the clifftop house.

'I'm going to be so fit and healthy after this is all over,' Susan laughed. 'Walking up and down the steep roads on this island is a great way to exercise.'

They went up to the front door, everything was quiet and the blue shutters on the upstairs windows remained shut. They only had to ring the bell once before the door was opened by Maria. She looked surprised to see them again. 'Mr. Saconne isn't here,' she answered in response to Aurelio's question. 'I don't think he will be back for several days, sir.'

'Maria,' Aurelio's voice was pleasant and soft. 'Maria, please tell me if my friend Angela is in this house. Did Mr Saconne bring her here, and is keeping her...maybe upstairs?'

'No! No!' she sounded frightened as she denied the question. 'No! She isn't here.'

Aurelio stepped further into the room. 'Where has my cousin gone, do you know?'

'No, he didn't say, just that he wouldn't be home until tomorrow, or the day after. He said I have to stay and look after the house. There's only me here, the other maid and the cook have been given time off.'

'That's strange, if he isn't coming back for a few days, why didn't he give you time off too? If the house is empty why do you have to stay?'

Maria looked confused and upset. 'I..I.... don't know. It's just what he said.'

As she was speaking, Susan noticed her eyes kept looking upwards.

'Why are you looking up there?' Aurelio asked. 'What's up there? I think we'd better go and look for ourselves.' He turned to Susan, 'come on, there's definitely something up there that is getting a lot of Maria's attention.

Time we had a look.' Susan and Aurelio started going up the stairs with Maria following behind, weeping and begging them not to go up there. When they reached the top, they saw a door on the right, at the beginning of a long passageway. When they tried to open it, they found it was locked.

'Open please, Maria,' ordered Aurelio. 'You have a key, open it or I'll kick it down. Imagine what your boss will say when he comes back and finds a broken door, at the very least he'll take it out of your wages, but knowing my cousin I think your punishment might be a lot worse than that.'

She looked so frightened by Aurelio's threats that Susan started to feel sorry for her. 'Come on, open it! I'm not asking again.'

She finally took a bunch of keys out of the pocket of her apron and slowly opened the door, then stood back and let Aurelio and Susan enter.

The first thing they saw was Angela lying on the bed. She was in such a deep sleep, only the rhythm of her breathing was an indication that she was alive. Aurelio stood over her, tears in his eyes. 'What has he done to her? What has that fiend done?'

His voice cracked with emotion. Susan put her hand on his shoulder to calm him. As they looked more closely, they saw a faint bruising on her wrist and a tiny prick mark which was inflamed around the edges.

'She's been drugged! God, that monster will pay for this! What should we do now? Is there a doctor on this island, there must be one? Maria do you know anyone? Is there a clinic close by?'

'Yes, there's a doctor, his practice is just down the road. I have his number downstairs.'

After ringing the doctor, Susan and Aurelio sat with Angela.

'I wonder how long ago he gave her the injection?' Susan asked. 'She might stay like this for hours. We need to get her away from here as soon as possible, before Peppino comes back. We should know more when the doctor comes. He should be here by now! Where is he?'

As soon as she said that, the loud peal of the doorbell echoed through the house. They could hear voices in the hallway, and then continuing up the stairs.

Dr Rossi was a tall thin man with a very intense expression. He seemed highly put out by this urgent summons to a house he regarded as a den of criminals. He had kept his distance from these neighbours after the owner of the house, the notorious psychopathic son of a mafia don, tried to force him to treat several of his men who were suffering from gunshot wounds.

He looked at Aurelio and Susan suspiciously. 'What is it?' Aurelio then explained that he was Peppino's cousin but had nothing to do with his business. He went on to tell the doctor that the girl was a friend of his who had been abducted by his cousin and that he had reason to believe she had been drugged. All he wanted was for the doctor to check that she was alright, and if she was, give them some indication of when she might wake up. He continued emphasising that he needed to get her out of this house and back to her family before his cousin returned.

The doctor looked calmer after his explanation, and proceeded to then check her carefully.

'Yes, she's been drugged,' he said eventually. 'An opioid, probably heroin and very pure. She's lucky she didn't overdose, and looking at her condition, I don't know if the person who gave it to her intended her to live.'

Aurelio and Susan looked at each other in shock.

'So it wasn't just a way of keeping her quiet until he got back, he wanted to keep her quiet permanently.'

The doctor continued, 'luckily she's strong and won't suffer any ill effects. Maybe a headache and some nausea, but nothing else. I don't think she should travel though; not yet anyway, we should wait until she wakes up naturally. If you don't think it's the best thing to stay here, we could take her to my house, it's just down the road.' Doctor Rossi packed up his bag and got ready to leave.

'I'll need to call her father first, then I'll get the car. Thanks for your help doctor, we'll be at your house soon.'

'I'll call the commissario,' Susan added. 'It's important that we let the police know too, don't you think Aurelio? Maybe they can put out an alert to watch for Peppino and arrest him. I'd feel a lot better if we knew he was in custody. Imagine if he came back and found us here. Who knows what he would do.'

Aurelio nodded. 'Yes I'll just make this call, and then we'll leave. I'd better see what's happened to Maria too. I wonder if she's still downstairs or done the wise thing and left?'

Susan could hear the sounds of joy and relief as Aurelio broke the happy news to Rocco Salvino. 'No, no don't come sir, she is safe and a doctor has checked her. We'll take her to his house and wait until she is awake and then we'll bring her to you. No, I don't know where Peppino is. We'll let the police know and they can take it from there. Yes sir, we'll see you soon,' and he finished the call.

The commissario took a little longer to answer Susan's call, he sounded stressed and official, but as soon as he heard her voice and her good news his voice softened. The relief that Angela had been found, and was safe, was evident in his response.

'That's wonderful news and she's ok? A doctor checked her, good, and you and Aurelio will take her back to her father? You don't have to worry about Peppino Saconne anymore, we found him dead at the family beach house in Santa Flavia. Shot in the back of the head. No sign of anyone else so I don't know what has happened to the rest of his coterie. I'll finish up here and come to Mr Salvino's home later. There are a lot of things that need to be cleared up, but now Angela's been found there isn't the same urgency. Thank you for letting me know, I'll be in touch later.'

'What's happened?' Aurelio asked.

'You wouldn't believe it, Peppino's dead. The police found him at his house in Santa Flavia, shot in the back of the head. Now we know that he won't be coming back here we don't have to leave straight away,' Susan said with relief. 'I know he was your cousin, Aurelio, but I am so glad he won't be around anymore. He was a really, dreadful, scary man.'

'No, we'd better go, we don't know why he was killed. We can't take the chance. Someone else might come, there may be others involved in Angela's kidnapping. They might come and take over the job, or finish it. Angela could be a witness. I don't think Peppino did this by himself. I think there were others involved.

We definitely need to go. I'll get the car and then come back and we'll try and get her down the stairs.'

It was awkward, half carrying, half lifting Angela's semi-unconscious body. As they carried her they could see that she was trying to come out of the drug induced fog. Her eyes flickered and some of her body's heaviness eased.

'Thank goodness, the drugs seem to be wearing off a bit,' Aurelio said with relief.

They spent the next hour at Doctor Rossi's house, while he kept an eye on Angela. When she finally came out of her drugged state, the surprise followed by joy, at seeing Aurelio and Susan, left her in tears of gratitude.

'You found me! I didn't think I would ever see you again.' She clung to Aurelio, her eyes filled with tears.

'That monster, what an awful creature. Where is he? Have they caught him? How did you find me? I had given up hope. I thought I was going to die.'

The questions tumbled out, there were so many. 'Shush, there's plenty of time to answer them. The most important thing is that you are safe. We've told your father and we're going to take you home. The other important thing that you need to know, and which will make you feel even better, is that Peppino is dead. He can never hurt you again.'

'Oh!' There was an immediate expression of relief, but nothing else.

'Oh Susan! It's great to see you too. Have you been helping Aurelio? Your Sicilian holiday has really turned into something quite different hasn't it?'

'It sure has. Never a dull moment around you lot. At least you are safe and well, that's the most important thing.'

'Are we ok to leave now, doctor?' Aurelio looked impatient to get going. 'I want to take her home.'

'Yes that's fine. I'm sure her family can't wait to see her.' Aurelio and Susan helped Angela to her feet. 'Thanks again for your help. I don't think there will be any more problems with your neighbours.'

After the ferry crossing, as they drove on towards Palermo, Angela turned to Aurelio.

'Why did you get a text about a meeting with Peppino? I saw it on your phone, when we were in Taormina. It frightened me. I thought you were mixed up with that gang. That's why I ran away to Savoca. Why were you meeting him, Aurelio?'

Chapter 20

The forensic team arrived promptly, along with other crime scene officers. Despite the initial shock, they dealt with this death following the usual routine. It would be accurate to say there were no feelings of pity at this crime scene, but rather a sense of relief. One less criminal to deal with, and a pretty dreadful one at that. There would be few who would mourn the death of Peppino Saconne.

As for Commissario Lombardo, first officer on the scene, he was still recovering from the shock and feeling an increasing puzzlement about the whole thing. One minute they were chasing down an unstable criminal and searching for a missing girl, then suddenly it was over, just like that. Angela had been found and was on her way back to her family. A likely tragedy had been averted, for there was no doubt in his mind that when Peppino Saconne returned, whether her father had agreed to his demand or not, Angela would have been given a final shot of heroin, strong enough to be fatal, then left behind for others to find like a discarded piece of rubbish. That was how those people worked. Leaving no loose ends behind. It seemed that anyone was expendable, even the mastermind.

'I'll need to go and see Don Saconne again,' he said to his two officers, Marino and Rizzo. 'I wonder if he knows yet?

I need to ask him some questions as soon as possible, before he has chance to concoct some story. Was the death of his son and heir a surprise? I wonder.....Did he know what his son was working on? I bet he did. Someone like him would certainly know what was going on in his family. That feeble, old man act doesn't fool me, not one bit. We know Peppino wanted to launder money through Rocco Salvino's bank and that he had something going on involving a Libyan businessman. It could be any number of things. Drugs, human trafficking, we know he has a finger in a number of pies. My question is, what was it that angered someone enough to kill him? I'm sure there are plenty of people who would love to see him dead, but who would have been brave enough, or stupid enough, to pull the trigger? The repercussions could be enormous. Gang warfare is a strong possibility. Can you imagine if it turns out to be someone from the Nigerian gang? We need to speak to Don Saconne and try and keep a lid on these tensions, which are certainly going to rise.'

The drive to Terrasini was uneventful and quick. There didn't seem to be much traffic so they arrived well before nightfall. No one was on duty at the heavy gates, but as they were slightly ajar and not locked, one of the officers got out and opened them up. They drove through and saw that no guards were patrolling the walls along the driveway.

The house looked deserted, and after they rang the doorbell, it took a very long time for anyone to answer. Finally, it was opened by the housekeeper. Her eyes were red rimmed and in her hand she held a crumpled handkerchief.

'Is the don at home?' She hesitated, then beckoned them in. 'He's in his study, sir,' and she led them to the door down the passageway where the commissario had been just a few days ago. She knocked gently, a voice replied..... 'come in.'

Lombardo didn't know what he expected to see. Certainly a man affected by grief, or at least mourning the sudden death of his only son. Don Saconne was sitting in a chair by an open window. He got up immediately when the commissario came in and walked towards him ready to shake his hand. Maybe he hadn't been told, although that was highly unlikely. 'Don Saconne, I'm sorry to be the bearer of bad news. It's your son, he's been found at the holiday house in Santa Flavia. He's dead, shot. I'm very sorry for your loss.' Lombardo stepped back slightly and watched the don's reaction.

Apart from a slight raising of his eyebrows and a look of mild surprise, he showed no other sign of shock, grief or anything else.

'Has someone already informed you?' Lombardo asked. 'Do you have any idea who was responsible for his death?'

'Yes, a contact I have in the Questura in Palermo called me and told me the news not long ago. I don't… don't know who was responsible, how would I know. I knew very little about my son's interests, he didn't confide in me and to be quite honest I already had misgivings about the way he had been conducting himself recently. I'm sure he had been taking drugs and it was having a detrimental effect on his behaviour of late. I'm deeply upset by what has happened, his sister is going to come from Germany tomorrow to help with the funeral arrangements. I really can't help you, Commissario, if I had any ideas I wouldn't hesitate to share them with you, but I am as puzzled by this as you are. Maybe he upset one of his business associates or someone was jealous. Sorry, I'm as much in the dark as you are.'

'It seems a rather extreme reaction to an unsatisfactory business deal,' Lombardo replied. 'Surely murder is not the way you show dissatisfaction over something like that?

Did you know he had abducted the daughter of Rocco Salvino and was holding her in his house on Levanzo? It was lucky your nephew and his friend found her and rescued her earlier today. Your son had drugged her and left her in a very perilous condition.'

'My son was an unstable man who did extreme things to get what he wanted. Nothing would surprise me about anything he did and the lengths he went to, to achieve them. I'm sorry Commissario, but I really am quite tired. I need to take a rest, if you don't mind. My son's death has taken quite a toll on my health and I am beginning to feel unwell. If you wouldn't mind, could you keep me updated with any information you find out in your investigation.'

He did look strangely flushed and preoccupied, so Lombardo took his leave, but not before delivering one last barbed comment.

'I'm sure your contact in the Questura will keep you updated on the investigation, Don Saconne,' and he left the room.

'How dodgy was he, sir?' one of the officers observed, as they walked back to the car.

'I'm sure he knows more than he's saying. That was a very low key reaction to the news, if you ask me.'

'Oh I think he's had quite a bit of time to think about what has happened,' Lombardo replied. 'He seemed like a man who'd had time to come to terms with the news.'

'Boss, who do you think his contact in the Questura is?' Marino asked.

'Well, I've got a few ideas, several people quite high up come to mind. Try not to worry about it, we have our job to do, and that is to find who murdered Peppino Saconne.'

'I wonder what happened to the guy who was with him, he never went anywhere alone, there was always a backup or two.

It's strange we didn't find another body at the house. Was he in on the hit, or got lucky and ran off, boss?'

'The killer or killers could have taken him, although it's unlikely. That would just be an added problem they wouldn't want to have to deal with,' Lombardo said thoughtfully.

'Let's go back to the office, go through what we have, then work out where we go from there. Rizzo, you can check the data base for known associates, business and otherwise. We need to get on to this right away before the trail goes cold on us. I also want to look at his apartment in Palermo and see if there's anything there that can help us. We should also call in and see Angela Salvino and her father. Rocco Salvino told me the reason Peppino took her was because he wanted to use his bank to launder money and also recommend one of his companies for some tender. He was using the daughter as leverage, a way of getting Salvino to agree. When he spoke to me, Salvino was adamant that he wouldn't do it but he was also desperate to find his daughter.'

'Do you think Angela's father could have killed Peppino, or got someone else to do it?' Officer Marino asked.

'I think that's highly unlikely, no matter how distressed he was, he isn't that sort of man, or doesn't strike me as being the type of man who uses violence as a way of dealing with problems.'

'But boss, don't you think some people can be driven to take matters into to their own hands, especially if they think the police aren't getting anywhere? It's happened before.'

'I agree, but not Rocco. He's never been a man to use violence for any reason. He's always tried to get results by using different methods. In his business dealings he is known for his cunning and out maneuvering rivals using clever strategies. He would be more likely to try and pit the criminals against each other to achieve what he wanted, not resort to violence and certainly not murder.'

As they pulled into the Questura car park it was obvious the news of Peppino Saconne's death had caused a buzz of activity. It was all anyone could speak about. Everyone had their own theories, which they didn't hesitate to share with the commissario.

A rival gang hit…. a jilted lover (Peppino wasn't married, and articles which focused on his many relationships were often featured in the tabloids), or business problems.

There were certainly plenty of reasons to get rid of Peppino Saconne, and any number of suspects who would have been willing to do it, especially if money was involved.

The meeting in the commissario's office didn't take long. Lists of duties were given out and a crime scene evidence board set up, then everyone went off to follow leads and check evidence. It would be a long night, but no one minded, they were all focused on finding the killer. The body was in the autopsy room and they were still waiting for the pathologist's results. Although it looked like a straightforward fatal gunshot wound, fingerprints, fibers etc. might help to find out who was responsible.

After returning to Peppino's apartment they used the keys and an attached remote control they had found in his car, to get through a veritable fortress of security. Lombardo and his men started going through the rooms not knowing what they were looking for but hoping something might jump out at them and provide the clue they so desperately needed. They hadn't been at it long when Marino gave a shout and came out of a room which seemed to be used as an office, waving a piece of paper. It was details of the shipment that had come from Russia. Lombardo remembered the conversation he'd had with the forklift driver when he was down at the docks the other day looking for Peppino. The most interesting thing about this document were the three names listed as importers of the farm equipment in the containers which were now sitting on the docks awaiting collection. Guiseppi Saconne, Don Saconne and Hassan Maziq.

Hassan Maziq, that must be Peppino's business partner, a shadowy figure who always managed to avoid close scrutiny. Although they had never been able to prove it, Lombardo suspected that he had been a backer in the organ trafficking debacle. If that was so, he would have lost a lot money and would certainly want to recoup it. Maybe this was Peppino's way of paying him back. There must be more to the deal than just farm equipment, that wouldn't be something that made you the amount of money that would satisfy those greedy men.

'I think we need to take control of those containers straight away.' Lombardo immediately rang the Questura and notified his superiors. 'We need to act quickly and search that farm equipment before someone takes the containers away. I'm sure they must have hidden something in the machinery. Every nut and bolt has to be unscrewed and gone over with a fine tooth comb. Take a couple of sniffer dogs too. I know there's something there. The idea of people like that bringing in farm machinery is ludicrous. Yes, sir, thank you, sir,' and he finished the call.

'Let's hope they get on to it straight away and impound those containers,' he said to his men. 'I don't want our investigation being hampered by someone at the top.'

Everyone was silent, but they all knew that this had happened before. Someone at the top, with too much to lose and questionable connections had lost the paperwork or forgotten to pass on orders. Fingers crossed that it wouldn't happen this time.

They continued with their search but apart from a stash of coke and a bag of pills, that would need to be tested, they found nothing else of importance.

'That's it then,' Lombardo said. 'Let's hope those containers give us something, then we can bring Don Saconne and the Libyan businessman in, and hopefully get some answers to the reasons behind Peppino's murder.'

'Come on, you owe me an explanation as to why you were having a meeting with Peppino,' Angela persisted. 'I'm waiting, Aurelio.' Her expression was one of determination and Aurelio knew that an answer would be necessary. She would never let it go otherwise.

Susan sat quietly in the back of the car. Aurelio had already given her an explanation, of sorts, but she knew it was between them and it would be unwise to interfere.

'I know it looks dodgy, but it wasn't. Peppino was trying to bully my father into doing some money laundering for him through his charity. He was threatening to cause problems, like disrupting some of the businesses he used, especially ones that supported jobs for refugees. He also said he would stop supplies of essential products like medicines. Dad was totally freaked out by the whole thing, the threats, the menacing phone calls. He tried to speak to his brother but he was useless. He just made excuses, saying things like, 'Oh, Peppino's his own man, I can't control him.'

'I decided to step in, and organised a meeting with him at the beach house. That's why that creep, Gianni, picked me up at the bus stop in Taormina. He was sniffing around looking for you, showing your photo around, and asking if anyone had seen you, so I had to get him off your trail. I also found out that they were covering all bases and were going to put pressure on your father as well. I didn't know where you were. I was out of my mind with worry, ask Susan or Commissario Lombardo. But when I saw Gianni I knew they didn't have you, so it gave me some time. That's why I organised the meeting, got Gianni to speak to Peppino and let him know I was coming to Santa Flavia straight away. It worked for maybe twenty-four hours, but after we met he realised I was just stalling and we had no intention of doing his dirty work. That's why they chose Plan B, tracked you down and abducted you. They turned their attention to your father instead. Peppino must have been really desperate and now he's dead.'

'But how did they know where I was? I didn't tell anyone except Susan, just so she didn't worry.'

'I didn't see that note until I came back to my room, after Aurelio had left with those men. I didn't tell anyone, except Commissario Lombardo and later, Angela's auntie. She was messaging me when Angela hadn't come back from her walk. She was out of her mind with worry. We know now that Angela had already been taken. Who could have known where you went? Maybe they had people tracking you down, you know, some people will do anything for money especially if they are poor, or unscrupulous people have something over them. Then they can use it to keep them under their control.'

Susan suddenly stopped talking. There was nothing more to say. It wasn't her job to try and work out what had happened and why, that was a job for the police. At least Angela was safe and Peppino was dead.

Angela seemed happy with Aurelio's explanation and so the rest of the journey continued with little conversation. Aurelio turned on the radio and chose some soothing music, this helped to calm them and by the time they were close to Angela's family home they felt relaxed and ready to face all the questions which were certain to be waiting for them.

'I think I'll get out here,' Susan said, just before they turned into Angela's street. 'I don't think I need to be there when you are reunited with your family. I feel a little awkward. This is a time for you and your family, and besides there are a few things I need to do. I haven't seen my friend Lucie for a few days, and she must be worried. I want to call her and then meet up. I'm so glad you're safe Angela. I'll come and see you soon.' And with that she grabbed her bag and got out of the car. Aurelio looked a little surprised by her sudden decision, but didn't try to stop her.

It was a relief to be alone and able to walk. Susan felt a sudden need to visit the cathedral. It wasn't far and so she headed down Corso Vittorio Emanuele. It wasn't too crowded and she was able to sit quietly at the back without feeling hemmed in. It really was a beautiful place. She often found herself coming here, especially when she needed some quiet time to think. The cathedral had originally been built in the twelfth century by the Normans on the site of a Saracen mosque, but over time there had been a number of alterations and restorations, including Gothic, Baroque and Neoclassical styles. Inside was a treasure trove of history, tombs, displays of jewels and beautiful artwork. You could also pass along a walkway across the roof and look over at the vast panorama of Palermo. But for now Susan was content to sit and relax. Just before leaving the stillness of the cathedral, she went first and lit a candle for one of her favourite people. Father Pino Puglisi, a murdered priest and teacher smiled down on all who passed. The cathedral housed the main shrine dedicated to him. There was a large photograph on display as well as a painting, which was new, and had been placed on an easel at the side of his tomb. His beautiful smile was captured forever, a reminder of this dear, gentle man who was violently gunned down in Brancaccio on his fifty-sixth birthday by a mafia hit man, in September 1993.

As she lit the candle, a strong smell of sweat mixed with tobacco assailed her nostrils. Before she could turn to see who it was, a rough voice spoke close to her ear, in broken English, 'donta look, justa listen. Someone says you gotta leave Palermo, hear me, you gotta leave, if you don something bad gonna happin.' There was a sharp push into her back, then the smell and the person disappeared. Father Pino gazed down, his kind eyes calming her shattered nerves. How hideous, Susan couldn't move, too frightened to turn in case he was lurking nearby. After some deep breathes and when she was sure the smell had gone, she gingerly looked sideways. Seeing nothing suspicious she then turned right around and walked quickly towards the main entrance. The gardens were ahead so she went straight away and sat on a seat trying to understand what had just happened. What an awful, creepy threat. Why on earth had that happened? Had she been mistaken for someone else? She didn't know anything. She thought immediately of messaging Commissario Lombardo and telling him what had happened. Why should she leave? Had she seen something that had upset someone, and who on earth was that someone? She sent a message to the commissario and within minutes her phone rang. As she told him briefly what had happened in the cathedral, she heard a sharp intake of breath.

'Stay where you are, I'll send a car, it will be alright,' and he was gone.

The police car came in a matter of minutes, he got out and came into the gardens.

'I didn't expect you to come, I'm sure you are busy, sorry... ..'Susan was surprised to see him. He sat down beside her on the bench.

'I felt I should, that was a truly awful thing to happen and in broad daylight, in a church of all places. I wonder how they knew where you were? They must have had a lookout or were following you.'

'Until a couple of hours ago I was in the car with Aurelio and Angela, we were bringing her back from Levanzo. I wanted to go to the cathedral first and then meet up with my friend Lucie. I didn't think there was any need for me to go to Angela's. That is a time for family. So after I got out of the car I walked along Corso Vittorio Emanuele and went straight inside. I didn't notice anyone watching me. I sat for quite a long time. It was only when I got up and lit a candle for Father Puglisi that the person came up beside me and started threatening me.'

'So you didn't get a look at him?'

'No, but I smelt him,' and Susan shuddered at the memory. 'He smelt strongly of tobacco and sweat. I think he hadn't shaved for a while either. I had the feeling, when he was whispering and his face was close to my ear, that I could feel stubble. I was so shocked that it's hard to remember much. If I remember more, I'll be sure to tell you.'

'I'll take you back to the Questura and you can make a report. We can't have people going around threatening others, especially foreign tourists. We are just beginning to enjoy the change of our past reputation. People feel Palermo is much safer now and we have been seeing record numbers of tourists visiting our beautiful city. This is not good. I don't want you being alone either. Are you still staying with your friend in Bagheria?'

'Yes, I've already messaged her. I'm going to meet her at the hotel where she works. I was going to go there after visiting the cathedral.'

'Right, that sounds perfect, so we'll take your statement and then I'll walk you to the hotel.'

Sitting in the commissario's office and going over her statement, Susan's thoughts kept returning to the reasons behind the shocking incident. She couldn't work out why someone wanted to harm her, and was determined to make her to leave. She racked her brains, trying to think of something she may have seen or heard that she shouldn't have.

She kept asking the commissario if he had any idea why this had happened and who could be behind it, but he was equally puzzled by the whole thing. All he could say was that it must be related to Angela's abduction or the massacre of the refugees. But there was the dead African too, you know the one I saw with those two men arguing and then he was killed later on.' The commissario looked thoughtful, 'yes, there is that too. You've certainly had an eventful holiday, that's for sure. At the moment the most important thing is keeping you safe, are you sure you'll be alright staying with your friend?'

'Yes I'm sure, and if I see anyone or anything that makes me feel uncomfortable, I'll let you know straight away.'

'Please be careful,' he said, shaking her hand outside the hotel, then he turned and walked back to the Questura.

Susan stood looking as he crossed the road, he really was such a dear sweet person, not at all how she imagined an Italian policeman to be. He certainly didn't fit any of the stereotypes common in books or movies.

Lucie was waiting for her in the lobby. She looked incredibly happy, her usual stressed expression now replaced by a relaxed one. She hugged Susan and led her to a table in the corner of the hotel's bar. 'Let's have a drink before we go. I've had some good news, and I can't wait to tell you.

I heard from my husband yesterday, and for some reason they are letting him come home. It was very sudden, but whatever he had done has been forgiven and he is free to come back to his family. After so long apart, it's hard to believe that this time next week he'll be here.'

'That's wonderful Lucie, really wonderful,' and Susan hugged her friend.

'Wow! I wonder what could have brought about this sudden change? But anyway, whatever it was, I'm so happy for you.'

It was really nice to finally be back in Bagheria and to be able to relax, knowing that Angela was safe. When they got home Susan filled Lucie in with the events that had taken place on Levanzo. 'It sounds just like a movie!' She kept exclaiming, shocked by the whole thing. 'What a holiday this has turned out to be. Happy seventieth birthday,' she laughed. Susan then told her about the scary encounter in the cathedral and her face changed. Shocked, she exclaimed 'Oh Susan, that's awful! You need to be careful. I hope the commissario will have some of his men close by, keeping an eye on you. Why would they be targeting you? You are just an innocent bystander in all this.'

'Well, they don't seem to think so, do they.' Susan smiled ruefully. 'Anyway tomorrow is a new day, and right now I'm exhausted.'

In the Questura, on Commissario Lombardo's desk, was a message that had come in from Lombardo's colleague, the coast guard in Malta, Matteo Vella. Lombardo had already left so he would not read it until tomorrow. The officer who had taken it from the internal telex machine didn't read it as they were short staffed and there wasn't any indication that it was urgent.

The message was passing on further information about the refugee boat they had discussed earlier. They had received further information, this time from an informant they used from time to time, who had links to several mafia families in Sicily. This boat was part of a larger people trafficking operation. They were not independent but part of a bigger business venture that had been set up by some major criminals. The boat would be arriving sometime in the next two days and judging by its route it was heading for the Egadi Islands. If he received more news he would send it on. He hoped it was helpful and they were able to act quickly.

Chapter 22

The next day, after a disturbed sleep filled with strange dreams which involved running through the streets of Palermo while being chased by unseen enemies, Susan went out early to get some pastries from the local bakery. She had just got to the end of Lucie's street and was waiting to cross the busy main road, when a fast moving car almost rode up onto the footpath and hit her. As she jumped back in fright she caught a glimpse of the driver and his passenger, they looked remarkably like the two men she had seen driving away from the Taormina bus terminal with Aurelio. The driver stared at her briefly and drew a finger across his neck, then they were gone. Several people came up to her, concerned about what had happened. 'Was she alright?' 'Did she need a doctor?' After reassuring everyone she was fine, she decided to give the pastries a miss and go back to Lucie's.

'You'll never believe what just happened, someone tried to run me down when I was walking to the shops. I'm sure they were the two men I saw with Aurelio in Taormina.' Susan sat down, feeling shaky.

'What! That's awful, I think we should ring the commissario, he would want to know about this. They are obviously doing their best to intimidate you. What a nightmare.' But just as

Susan was about to make the call, her phone started to ring. It was Angela. 'Hi Susan, hope all is ok. I just wondered if you wouldn't mind driving back to Levanzo with me. I know it's a big ask but I can't get hold of Aurelio and I don't want to go alone. I left a jacket there that I really love. Now that I know Peppino won't be coming back I don't think there'd be a problem if I called in, just for a short while. It won't take long and we could stop and have lunch. It's a beautiful day and it might be nice to relax after everything that has happened.'

'Are you sure you are ready to go back there?' Susan asked. 'Won't it freak you out? It was only yesterday that you were rescued. Wouldn't it better to wait for a few days?'

'No, if I wait someone might take the jacket, it's expensive, Dolce and Gabbana. My parents gave it to me for my birthday so I want to get it as soon as possible. If you don't want to come, that's ok. I'll just go by myself.'

'No, no I'll come with you, I don't want you going by yourself. I'm staying at my friend's house in Bagheria so I'll have to catch the train to Palermo, can you wait for me?'

'I'll come and get you, it's the least I can do. I'm just leaving my house now, so I shouldn't be too long. Text me the address and I'll see you soon.'

'Well, I'm not sure if you caught that, Angela left a jacket at Peppino's house on Levanzo and she wants to drive there and get it. She can't get hold of Aurelio and so she wants me to go with her. I can't seem to get away from that place. I used to love it, but now I'm not so sure.' Susan grimaced.

'Are you sure you want to go, especially after what just happened?'

'Well, I'll be in a car with someone, so I won't be alone. I'm sure I'll be fine. It's just there and back with a stop for lunch.

It's around three hours there and three hours back, so I should be back late afternoon.'

'That sounds fine. I just heard from my husband and he'll be coming tonight or early tomorrow.' Lucie looked excited, but also a little worried. 'I wasn't expecting him until next week, and now, suddenly, he tells me he'll be arriving sooner. I'll have to clean up a bit and let the children know. Everything is happening so quickly, it's hard to get my head around it. I'll have to ring work now and see if they can get someone to cover for me. Ah! So much to do.' She gave Susan a hug. 'Let me know how you go, and keep your eyes open for dodgy, sweaty men who smoke.'

'Are you sure you really want to do this?' Susan asked, as they drove out of town on the freeway towards Trapani. 'You don't think visiting that house could trigger some anxiety Angela? You know the mind and body can play tricks on us, especially if we've been through a severe traumatic event. It was only yesterday that you were drugged and lying in that house.'

'I think it might actually make things better, like facing your fears, anyway my focus is getting that jacket,' Angela laughed. 'I wonder where Aurelio is? He said he was going to check in this morning but so far no word. I tried to ring him a couple of times but he's not answering. It's a bit strange.'

'I bet your family were happy to see you back safe and sound, they must have been so worried.'

'Yes, they were, crying and hugging me, treating Aurelio like a hero. It was a bit much, but I can understand their relief, I was happy too. Peppino was insane. Imagine thinking that my father would agree to launder money for him. It was such a crazy idea.'

'But what if we hadn't found you, what do you think he would have done?'

'I really don't know. I don't want to think about it. But anyway, it's over, and we don't have to wonder, thank goodness.'

Commissario Lombardo had come into work early and found the message from Matteo Vella on his desk. He cursed that he hadn't stayed a bit later the day before, instead of leaving early, but it was too late for regrets. There was a lot to do. He needed to check in with the men who had gone to open the containers at the docks. They had only left an hour ago and he hoped they weren't having any problems. He knew there were drugs packed into the machinery, but it was time consuming looking for them. The traffickers were getting very inventive with their hiding places so it was always a challenge trying to keep up with them. He would have gone with them, but now, as well as Peppino's murder, he had the imminent arrival of a boat load of refugees.

Peppino's murder was interesting. It didn't appear to be random, in fact it looked as if someone had got sick of his behaviour and wanted to put an end to it. Lombardo had the very strong feeling that soon, all would be revealed. Instead of searching for a killer, when the time was right, the killer would come forward with an explanation.

Now he needed to go to the Egardi islands. Out of the three islands, he thought Levanzo was the most obvious choice. Favignana was bigger, and crowded at this time of year. Marettimo, was the most isolated and logistically harder to make the necessary arrangements to move the refugees on. He decided to take three carloads of men and have medical support staff standing by. He thought at this point the less fuss the better. He didn't want to draw attention to what was going on. To be honest, he was still haunted by two things, the trafficked children he and his men had rescued from Santa Flavia and the massacred refugees from Isola Bella. If he could bring these people to safety it might just go a little way in making him feel less helpless.

The men were ready and armed, in case there was a problem. Considering what had happened before, they were taking no chances. Focused and resolute, they headed out of the carpark and on towards Levanzo.

Susan and Angela made good time and arrived on Levanzo around two pm. Their plan was to go straight to Peppino's house, get the jacket, then find a place to have lunch.

'What if there's no one there to let us in?' Susan asked. 'What do we do then? Have you thought of that, Angela?'

'Maria should have a key, if she's not there we can easily find out where she lives.' Angela didn't seem particularly worried by the potential problem.

They drove up and parked. The place looked deserted. Angela rang the bell and waited. After a few minutes the door was opened by an elderly woman.

'Hello, I'm Angela, I left my jacket here yesterday, and I was wondering if I could come in and get it, if that's ok? I'll only take minute.'

The woman stared at her for a moment, then stood aside to let them pass.

'Where is Maria?' Angela asked as she went through into the hallway.

'Gone, and good riddance, left without saying anything!' The old woman sneered. 'The house was left unattended. Don Saconne sent me here from his house, to take care of things until they work out what to do.'

Angela went quickly up the stairs into the room where she had been held captive. Surprisingly, she didn't feel any ill effects, not even the slightest anxiety, which was a relief. At first she couldn't see the jacket and her hopes fell. I bet Maria took it, she thought. But as she went to leave, she caught sight of it, half hidden under the bed. Grabbing it gratefully, she headed back down the stairs again. 'Found it!' She held the jacket up, showing it to Susan. 'That's lucky, I thought maybe Maria had taken it.' Me too, Angela concurred, 'but it was under the bed, so thankfully she didn't see it.'

They thanked the woman and then left.

'That didn't take long, let's go and have lunch. I'm so glad I've got my jacket. I feel better already.'

They found a trattoria nearby, which was built almost over the water. The wide open windows let in a cool sea breeze. Gazing at the peaceful view of white cliffs and the blue water was just what they needed. Although it was busy, it wasn't noisy. Everyone was focused on eating the delicious looking food. There was an empty table near a window so they indicated to the waiter they would like to sit there. After ordering some antipasti and two plates of mussels in a spicy tomato sauce, they sat back enjoying a welcome Aperol Spritz.

'Sitting here makes you forget everything, doesn't it?' Susan said.

'Yes, it does, I wish we could sit here day after day, just enjoying the food and the view,' Angela agreed.

They were half way through their meal when they heard the sound of several cars roaring up the hill. When they looked, they saw three police cars. In the one leading was a man who looked like Commissario Lombardo.

'Did you see that? Was that who I think it was?' Susan gasped. They both looked shocked. 'I wonder what is going on? Why are they here do you think?'

'Maybe it's something to do with Peppino's death, they're heading up that way. I think I'll message him and tell him we're here. I'm sure he would want to know, and that old woman might tell him we were there earlier.'

'That's true,' Angela nodded in agreement.

As soon as Susan sent the message her phone started ringing.

'Hello,' the commissario's voice sounded stressed. 'What on earth are you two doing here? This is not the best place for you to be at the moment. We've got an important operation that's about to start. It could also be dangerous.'

Susan then explained why they had come, and without thinking, added to the commissario's stress by telling him about the car that had nearly run her over earlier. When she mentioned that she had recognised the two people in the car as the men she had seem with Aurelio in Taormina, he became very quiet.

'Right, I don't want you and Angela going back to Palermo now. I think it's better if you stay here until this is all over. We are up at Peppino's house. We are going to use it as a base for the time being, so you should come straight here after you've finished eating. I'll explain more when you get here. Please, keep on your guard, there are some strange things going on here at the moment. Stick together and don't let each other out of your sight.'

'Wow! This day is getting crazier and crazier,' Susan said, after she had finished speaking to the commissario. 'There's something big going on and he doesn't want us to go back to Palermo yet. We have to go back to Peppino's house when we've finished lunch. They are using it as a base for the operation they're involved with.

Angela looked concerned, 'I wonder if Aurelio knows what's going on? I still haven't been able to get hold of him. It's not like him to ignore my calls and messages. I hope nothing has happened to him. After everything that has gone on, his cousin's death, the don's strange behaviour, it's all a bit much. Even though his cousin was awful, when they were young they were close. They spent a lot of time together, almost like brothers, not cousins, but then when they got older and their families took different paths, they fell out. But they always say blood is thicker than water, so I think Peppino's death has affected him more than he has let on.'

Chapter 23

High up on the cliff, in the house which had until recently, belonged to the late Peppino Saconne, there was a buzz of activity and a barely suppressed feeling of nervous anticipation. Men were setting up surveillance equipment, including a strong telescope that could follow what was happening far out to sea.

When Susan and Angela reached the house, the old woman let them in again. She seemed nonplussed by the police presence.

'Does Don Saconne know you are using his house?' Angela asked Commissario Lombardo, as he came into the room from the terrace to meet them.

'Of course, I told him we had to go through Peppino's things to see if we could find any evidence of who had killed him, he was happy to go along with that.'

'But that's not all that's going on, is it?' she replied. 'It looks far more complicated than that.'

'Well, yes, it is,' and the commissario went on to tell them about the message he had received from the Maltese coast guard and what they were doing to save the people on the rapidly approaching boat.

'Hopefully, we can get to them before the traffickers do. This is a chance to make things right and give those poor souls an opportunity to have a better life.'

'That's amazing, I hope it all goes well. I see you have plenty of people here to help and we are here as well now, so if there's anything we can do, please don't hesitate to ask.'

'Thank you Susan, I have to tell you how shocked and angry I was after you told me about the car that tried to run you over this morning. One of the men sounds like Gianni. I'm sure you remember him. You have unfortunately crossed paths quite a few times during your holiday. A nasty character. I also want to speak to him about Peppino's murder. From what people have told me, he was with Peppino at the house in Santa Flavia. After we found Peppino I was surprised not to find Gianni's body there as well. But now that he has been seen several times since it happened, it makes me wonder if he could have had something to do with it, or someone paid him to look the other way.'

'You haven't, by any chance, seen Aurelio?' Angela asked. 'I have been ringing and leaving messages but he hasn't replied. I haven't seen him since he dropped me off at my parents' house yesterday. I hope he's alright and nothing bad has happened to him.'

'No, I haven't, but I'd like to speak to him too. When our officers went to impound some containers at the docks this morning, a consignment that had been brought in by Peppino and several of his business partners, we were told that Aurelio and another man had gone there earlier. They were trying to arrange for the containers to be moved to a building out of town, an abandoned factory, close to the town of Terrasini. It is a very strange coincidence isn't it. The fact that it is so close to

Don Saconne's house makes me wonder how involved he is as well. When I spoke to him a few days ago he denied knowing what Peppino was up to. Then after Aurelio and his mate were told it had already been impounded by the police as part of the investigation into Peppino's death and that they would have to wait until everything had been checked, they looked very angry and left pretty quickly. 'We believe, that hidden inside the machinery, are drugs that have been brought in from Russia. We have to pull everything apart. It's a long, tedious job but we know they are there. Peppino's name was on the paperwork and now he's dead, that makes things complicated.

I have to admit I was surprised to find out that Aurelio turned up, I didn't think he had anything to do with that side of the family business.'

'Neither did I,' Angela said, puzzled by his comments.

'Commissario, now do you think his explanation about being with Gianni and that other man at the bus terminus in Taormina, adds up. He said he was trying to help his father. He always seems to be where the action is, but with a ready answer to any questions as to why he is there. I've had my suspicions about him for a while, that's why I didn't tell him I was going to Savoca. I just had a feeling that he couldn't be trusted. Yet when I confronted him, he made out that I was overreacting and making a fuss over nothing. He was very quick with reasonable answers, and after he rescued me I thought, of course he is a good person and not involved in that family's crimes. It seems my fears were justified after all.'

The rest of the afternoon passed quickly. Everyone was on tenterhooks, ready to spring into action, while at the same time keeping an eye on the calm sea in front of them. In the background was constant static from the radio sending out updates as they continued to wait for a sign of the approaching boat. It was almost twilight and the encroaching darkness meant that their tactics had to change slightly. Strong lights were set up on the terrace, which brightened the way, and gave the officers a clear view of where the boat would land.

At eight-thirty, the light from a small boat, heading towards the harbour, was finally picked up. There was a general feeling of relief that it had reached safety after it's long journey. But it was not over yet. Looking through the telescope you could see there were men, women and children on board. They all looked to be in reasonable health, as far as it was possible to see from that distance.

It was time to move, the moment they had all been waiting for. Commissario Lombardo gave the order and he and the other officers' put on their vests, picked up their guns and silently made their way down to the harbour. He was leading with his two deputies following close behind. Several medics went with them, carrying bags of medical supplies. A couple of officers stayed at the house, still monitoring the boat through the telescope and preparing support for after the rescue was complete. They kept up a constant conversation detailing the boat's onward movement through their walkie talkies.

'Why do they need weapons?' Susan asked. 'What do they think is going to happen, surely they aren't in any danger now?'

'Who knows,' Angela replied. 'Maybe they don't want what happened in Taormina to happen again. There might be people lurking somewhere close by, waiting to attack. These boats don't come out of the blue. The whole thing is well planned. They want to use those people for any number of reasons. Maybe this boat is just landing here because that's where it ended up, but I don't think so. I suppose they don't want to take any chances. Hopefully everything will run smoothly and they won't need the guns.' It was, as if by uttering those words,

Angela tempted fate. A few seconds later several shots rang out directed at the boat, which was now almost in the harbour.

In the distance, Susan and Angela could see the boat's passengers cowering down, sheltering from the bullets. There was a return of fire, then silence. The women looked at each other in horror.

'What on earth is happening out there?' They looked towards the remaining officers for an explanation.

'The gunfire is coming from somewhere close by,' one of them replied, as he picked up a weapon. 'You two better go inside, it's dangerous out here and you aren't protected.'

They moved inside, but at the same time there was a crash downstairs, as the front door smashed open. They could hear the sound of heavy footsteps moving up the stairs. Breathing heavily and looking incredibly angry, Aurelio stormed into the living room holding a high powered rifle. Susan and Angela stared at him in astonishment.

'Aurelio, why are you here?' Angela managed to ask. 'I've been trying to get in touch with you all day.'

He stared back at them, 'I could ask you the same thing, why are you here?'

It was an Aurelio they didn't recognise. He now looked more like Peppino, mean and threatening. Their instincts warned them to be careful and not to make him angrier. He looked unstable and dangerous.

'It's good to see you, Aurelio,' Angela attempted to calm him. 'I came here looking for my jacket. I found it thank goodness. It was so expensive. I would have been really sad if I hadn't come back and got it. Remember, my parents gave it to me for my last birthday, you were there. Things were such a mess yesterday that I totally forgot to take it with me,' and she rattled on and on.

Although he was staring at her, they could see he wasn't really listening, his mind obviously on other things.

'We were going to leave as soon as we got the jacket, but Commissario Lombardo thought it was better that we stayed here until they had rescued the people on the boat. Did you see the boat? Aaah!' Angela suddenly became quiet. Of course he had seen the boat that's what he had been shooting at. What a fool I am, she thought, but this was no time to stop, and she continued talking.

'He felt we weren't safe driving back to Palermo, that it was dangerous if we left, so here we are. You can't argue with a policeman, can you?' She gave a nervous laugh. 'But I really would like to know why you're here Aurelio?' Angela asked again. 'And with a gun. I didn't know that you even knew how to use one. I think you owe me an explanation; don't you agree?'

'This hasn't gone the way we planned. It wasn't meant to go like this.' He looked sad and confused, but then suddenly turned angry again. 'You and your busybody friend shouldn't be here. Now you've got yourselves caught up in a situation that's got nothing to do with you. Why couldn't you have bloody well left? Why did you choose today of all days to come here? It's turned into a bloody horrible mess. I love you Angela, I thought one day we might get married. Imagine how powerful our families would be. Your father's money and my family's business connections. What am I going to do now? I have people waiting for the merchandise and I can't deliver it. I'm done for. These people are really dangerous, they won't accept no, for an answer. They have already lost money, this was my last chance to placate them and now it's failed.' He started punching the wall and sobbing.

'Are you talking about the people on the boat? Aurelio please don't tell me you are involved in this. Why? I can believe

Peppino was, but not you. You aren't like him, you're a good person. What has made you change and become part of this?' Angela started crying.

Aurelio stopped punching the wall and turned to them. 'I had to do it, Peppino was crazy, he was causing problems for certain people. Men you can't cross and who expect quick returns from their business investments. His crazy behaviour, especially towards the Nigerian gangs in the Mercato, was drawing unnecessary attention to his business interests and him. The people who'd made substantial investments in his projects didn't want that sort of attention. They were threatening to destroy my father's charities. I couldn't let that happen. I'm also a Saconne, it's now up to me to carry on and deliver on my uncle's commitments. The family shame would be too much. We've already suffered a massive loss and now it looks like we are going to lose even more. This could mean the end for us and I don't know how to fix it.' He started sobbing again. Angela and Susan looked at him in disgust. 'You're pathetic Aurelio, really pathetic! You'll just have to deal with the consequences. I hope your poor father can be protected. You've certainly got yourself involved with some dreadful people. What did you expect? You've seen enough surely, to know what happens if you don't deliver.....'

Another set of footsteps were coming up the stairs. Maybe it was some of the officers returning. They turned expectantly, as a fat, sweaty Gianni, his red, hostile face looking even angrier, when he saw Susan standing there, burst in, shouting.

'Not you again, interfering puttana!' He spat out the insult as he came closer. 'You bitch,' he lunged at her and slapped her face, his spittle landing on Susan's cheek. She smelt the sweat and tobacco and saw the stubble on his dark face, and she knew without a doubt that it was the same person who had whispered those threats in her ear at the cathedral yesterday. Surprisingly she felt strong and not afraid at all. She stepped back out of his way. Angela then took hold of her arm and pulled her closer.

Gianni continued his rant, ' dinna you get the message? How many times do I have to warn you? I shooda finished you off once and for all today. I'ma not gonna to make the same mistake again.' Angela and Susan moved further in the direction of the terrace, towards the officers who they knew, were out there.

'Stop! You stupid, bloody cow!' he cursed, and he pulled a large knife from his belt. 'It'l be nice and quick, donna you worry,' and he moved closer. Susan had shut her eyes, waiting for a miracle. She could feel Angela's hand and she was comforted. Where on earth were those officers? Couldn't they hear what was going on. But before he could reach her a shot rang out. Susan opened her eyes and saw him fall, jerking at her feet. Blood splattered over her face and clothes and continued spreading quickly, until it covered almost all of Gianni's shirt. One of the officers came into the room and stopped, a shocked look on his face. 'What the hell happened here?' He stared down at Gianni's blood soaked body. 'Bloody hell, it's Gianni. We heard voices, but we thought it was the TV,' he then turned and stared in disbelief at Aurelio standing there, a rifle in his hand. 'What is he doing here? What just happened?' The other officer who had come in after him went and took a closer look at the body, lying motionless on the floor. 'That's Gianni isn't it? Fancy that! I wonder what he has to do with this? No great loss though. He's caused the police more headaches than anyone has a right to. Why are you here Aurelio? Are you here with Gianni or checking on these two women?' He then looked at Susan, her face and clothes covered in smears of blood. 'Signora, are you alright?'

'I'm fine officer, I'm not hurt. It's not my blood.'

Aurelio was standing there muttering ....'I couldn't let him hurt them, I just couldn't. He had to be stopped,' and he dropped the gun on the floor.

'Easy sir, calm down,' one of the officers picked up the gun and put it out of the way.

Aurelio looked at the ground, 'I came here to check on my cousin's property. My uncle, Don Saconne sent me, that man was his driver, he drove me here,' he pointed to Gianni's body.

'Well you need to stay here. We have a rescue going on at the moment. Are you sure you aren't here to meet the boat? It wouldn't be one of Don Saconne's business interests that you are here to look after, would it?'

Aurelio's previous expression of indignation was replaced by a shifty one. Susan and Angela both noticed he was refusing to meet anyone's eye and seemed to be fixated on the door leading out onto the terrace.

'I'm sure Commissario Lombardo will want to speak to you as soon as he's finished at the harbour, I know he's got a lot of questions he'd like to ask you.'

The officer took out a pair of handcuffs and fastened him to a chair. 'Just in case you don't feel like staying,' and he went back to his watch.

'The people are landing now. This is a good outcome for us and them,' he called out to Susan and Angela.

'Do you think it would be ok if we went down?' Susan asked the officer. 'I think the danger has passed. We'll keep out of the way. I just feel after everything that has happened it would be good to be there and help if it's needed. I saw there are small children and several babies. I'm good with children. I think I could be useful down there.'

At first the officer looked doubtful. 'I should really run it past the boss,' he said uncertainly, but the radio kept crackling and he seemed under a lot of pressure, so as soon as he had given them a tentative 'oh go ahead then,' and turned back to his work, Susan and Angela quickly left the house before he could check with the commissario, and headed down the long steep road towards the harbour.

Chapter 24

When Susan and Angela finally reached the wharf, it was abuzz with activity. The boat had docked and the refugees were being helped onto dry land. People from several relief agencies, as well as medical personnel and of course the police, were assisting them. Susan's eyes filled with tears. There were already several groups of people sitting patiently on the dock. As she looked at them their faces seemed familiar. A wave of emotion swept over her. Had it only been a week since she had found the bodies of the murdered refugees? It seemed much, much longer. These were the lucky ones. She and Angela came forward and started to help the mothers carrying babies and small children. Susan picked up a small boy, rugged up in a coat and blankets and hugged him to her.

'Hello, what an adventure you've had, welcome to Sicily.' The child looked at her gravely, it's big brown eyes solemn and watchful. She was sure he couldn't understand a word she said, but he seemed to know she was a friend. As Susan placed him into the arms of one of the relief workers, she was glad to see him return a little smile.

On she went, to the next one, and the next. Comforting them and making sure they were looked after. She and Angela helped through the night. Once each person had left the boat and been given a quick medical examination, they were wrapped in blankets and then given food and water. A bus would then take them to the processing center in Palermo.

Susan could see Commissario Lombardo standing a little away from the intense activity. He was looking out to sea, an expression of relief on his tired face. She went up to him and put her hand on his sleeve.

'Signora Susan, how glad I am to see you here. Are you alright? I heard there was a dangerous incident back at the house. I was going to come back but the officers there assured me that the threat had been dealt with successfully.'

'Yes, Gianni and Aurelio came to the house, then that dreadful Gianni attacked me with a knife. It was awful. Thank goodness Aurelio had the moral sense to shoot him, before he could hurt me. Gianni kept saying that he should have finished me off this morning in Bagheria. God I'm glad he's dead! He really was a shocker! What a hideous, violent man!' Susan shuddered, just thinking of those threats, and how close she'd come to being another of his victims, made her feel sick. Lombardo looked across at her. Concerned, he put his arm around her shoulders and gave them a gentle squeeze.

'I'm so sorry you got involved in all of this. You came here to have a holiday in beautiful Sicily and look at what has happened to you over the last week.

First, you found the boat with those poor murdered people, then you had the added misfortune to come across the stabbed African near the bus depot. After that there was Angela's kidnapping, those terrible threats in the cathedral and the attempted hit and run in Bagheria. To top it all off, just a few hours ago that brutal man tried to kill you. I would be surprised if you ever wanted to visit Sicily again. I am so, so sorry Susan.'

They stood quietly for a few more minutes until one of the officers interrupted the peace.

'We're finishing up here now sir, the migrants are on their way to Palermo, but there's still the problem up at the house. What do you want us to do with Aurelio? We can get the ambulance to take Gianni's body back to Palermo, but do you want to come and question Aurelio now, or back at the Questura?'

'There are so many questions we need answers to. I'll come back to the house with you, but we'll save the interrogation for later. What is Aurelio's involvement in this? That's the question I'd really like an answer to.'

He turned back to Susan, 'well, it looks like our quiet moment is over for now.'

There was a reluctance, from both of them, to go their separate ways.

'Before you go, I just wanted to thank you for all your effort in coordinating this rescue. I feel that finally, some good has come after the dreadful events in Taormina. Looking at those people and seeing their happiness and relief after finally reaching a safe shore, gave me a feeling of such joy.... and closure in a way. I know the others didn't make it, but at least these people will have a chance. Did I ever tell you about the nun I met on the train to Sampieri? She was from Cambodia and worked with refugees in Syracuse. After everything that's happened, it's made me think that I'd like to go there when this is all over, and volunteer. I'm a teacher, so I'm sure there would be something useful I could do.

The commissario smiled. 'Yes Susan, I agree. That sounds like a great idea. Although what happened in Taormina was dreadful, and we can't bring those people back, there are others who need our help. I think that is a great idea to go to Syracuse for a while. Goodness knows after what these people have been through they deserve every chance to make a good life for themselves. Even as we speak there are more boats coming, full of people seeking a better life. All we can do is try and give them the opportunity, however small it is. In the end it will be up to them. I'll go now, and deal with Aurelio. Hopefully, I'll get some answers. Would you mind calling in at the Questura later today? I'll need to get a statement from you about Gianni's attack.'

'Of course,' spontaneously, she gave him a hug. Thank you, again. I'd better go and find Angela or I'll miss my ride back to Palermo. To think we only drove here to pick up her jacket and have lunch.' She laughed. 'See you this afternoon.'

There was little conversation as Susan and Angela drove back to Palermo, both of them deep in thought, reliving the events in the house and afterwards down at the harbour.

'I can't get over Aurelio! You know I always felt uneasy around him. I told you that didn't I? But to be a part of that family's business, involved in all those awful things, people smuggling, drugs ... What a creep! It just goes to show; you can't change who you are, can you? Genetics are genetics I suppose. I'm just so disappointed in him. Would you believe he was studying criminology too. What a joke!'

'Oh Angela! I can understand how disappointed you are, but at least he saved you from Peppino, he didn't leave you in the house, and he saved me too. If he hadn't shot Gianni, goodness knows what would have happened to me. Ugh! I hate thinking about it. I don't think he knew that Peppino was behind your kidnapping, unless it was just a ruse. He does care about you, just not as much as he cares about Don Saconne. I think he wanted to be the heir. Peppino was unstable and causing so many problems, he had become too much of a liability. Later, we'll have to go and give our statements. I hope Commissario Lombardo has some answers for us then.'

'I think he has a soft spot for you, Angela looked across at Susan. 'You both seemed very relaxed, standing there looking out to sea.'

'Ha, ha, ha,' Susan laughed. 'I think we were both tired and overwhelmed by everything that had happened. It was just nice to stand there in silence. I also think he was worried after Gianni attacked me, in case I had delayed shock or something, but he is a dear person isn't he?'

'Yes, he is,' Angela agreed. 'He's definitely not your average policemen.'

'We're nearly in Bagheria, I'll pick you up later this afternoon and we can go to the Questura together.'

'Thanks so much Angela, we've been through a lot together haven't we? I know I'll be glad to get to the other side of all this, but I would also like some answers too.'

'Me too, see you later then.......'.

Susan opened the door to Lucie's apartment, trying to make as little noise as possible. She needn't have worried. Lucie was up and her husband was just making some coffee.

'How wonderful, you are finally home Giovanni. Lucie, you must be so happy.'

Lucie had the biggest smile on her face and so did her husband. Hopefully this would be the beginning of a better life, but there was still the mystery of why he had suddenly been allowed to return to Sicily. It was so unexpected, but maybe it was best to leave things be, and not delve too deeply into the reasons why.

'Where have you been Susan?' Lucie looked at her questionably. 'It's almost daybreak.'

'Oh Lucie! What a day it turned out to be, I hardly know where to begin...... You know how Angela and I were going to Levanzo to pick up her jacket, well.......' Susan sat, retelling the events of the day before. Lucie and her husband sat open-mouthed as she told the incredible story. Surprisingly she felt better going over what had happened. It now seemed like a distant memory and not as raw and terrifying as it had been. It was as if she was talking about someone else.

When she had finally finished, Lucie got up and hugged her. 'How brave you were Susan; I am in awe of you.'

Her husband's reaction was slightly different.

'Giovanni, isn't Susan brave? What an incredible woman, don't you think?'

'Yes, yes, she is. Yes, you are, Susan, what an incredible story.'

Although he was making an effort to appear concerned, expressing gratitude that she had escaped a horrible fate at the hands of a dangerous hit man, his behaviour was a little strange. He was having a hard time looking at her, and on the rare occasions that he did catch her eye, he looked quite shifty, as if he knew far more about the whole thing than he was giving away.

'I suppose a lot of those boats would pass by Malta? I've heard that they're not particularly welcoming there, and the coast guard and Libyan authorities often work in collusion to stop the boats, then escort them back into Libyan waters. It doesn't seem fair does it?'

'No, no, I try and keep out of things like that, Susan. I'm just a humble businessman trying to make a living, nothing else. I don't get involved. Well I need to have a lie down. I hope I see you later Susan,' he said, quickly changing the subject. ..... 'By the way, how long are you staying?'

'I'll leave tomorrow. Later today I have to go and give a statement at the Questura in Palermo. Angela will pick me up and we'll go together. I'll catch the bus to Ragusa tomorrow morning and then go on to Cava D'Aliga.I'll stay there for a couple of days, then I plan on going to Syracuse and help the refugees at a centre there. I met a nun recently who works at the centre so I'll ring her soon and arrange to go there and maybe teach English or whatever they need me to do. After what's happened over the last week I really feel this is what I need to do. Good night Giovanni, goodnight, Lucie.'

As she got ready to have a rest Susan couldn't help thinking about Giovanni. I wonder why he's been allowed to come back? I hope he doesn't hurt Lucie again. The whole thing seemed a little strange. The sooner she was out of here the better.

Chapter 25

Angela had picked up Susan at two o'clock. Although they were both tired, the fact that they might finally get some answers, invigorated their flagging energy. Now they were sitting in Commissario Lombardo's office going over the events from the day before. After completing their statements, they now waited expectantly for the commissario to explain the reasons behind the events of the past week.

He looked at them both, fondly, his hands fiddling with the sheaf of papers in front of him.

'So, let's start at the beginning, shall we? We will say that it all began with the massacred refugees. Everything that came afterwards can be linked back to that violent act. Their journey had been organised by a group of people who specialise in human trafficking, which in turn, supplies several markets. The main ones being, slave labour, prostitution and organ harvesting. What we have to understand is that those people were doomed, from the moment they stepped onto the boat. The group, who had organised their passage were from Libya and Sicily and had markets ready and waiting. The problem was, there was a power conflict between Peppino and his father. His father had organised the boat but made the mistake of putting Peppino in charge. His erratic behaviour began to cause problems with the Libyan backer. He complained to Don Saconne and threatened to withdraw his money if something wasn't done about Peppino. When Don Saconne confronted Peppino, he organised with some of his close allies to get rid of the boat and people, in revenge. Those people were murdered because of the out of control ego of a crazy person....'

'And the dead African in Taormina, how did he fit into the picture?' Susan asked.

'That unfortunate person had been part of a group who was meant to take some of the refugees to work in the market gardens. He hadn't been paid and made the mistake of complaining. Gianni soon put a stop to that, permanently. We have to assume that, anyway, because we aren't going to get any answers from a corpse.'

'That sounds right,' Susan said ruefully. 'He was certainly responsible for a lot of deaths, including nearly mine.'

'Yes, he was a really nasty piece of work. He also killed a Nigerian youth and cut off the ear of another one, the boy you saw being taken off the bus. Luckily he survived and is now in a safe place recovering. Peppino had become a liability and his father knew he had to do something about it before it impacted on his numerous business ventures. There was a shipment of drugs that had been hidden in some farm machinery, which was to be used to pay back the Libyan backer who had lost money when Peppino ordered the deaths of the refugees. The sale of the drugs was meant to appease his growing anger, and also finance the next deal. Peppino was killed before he could cause any more problems. The execution was ordered by Don Saconne. He had already persuaded Aurelio to take his place. I think he had been working on him for a while and Aurelio felt special being singled out as the don's future successor.'

'So the don was responsible for killing his own son? How awful. What a dreadful man. I thought he was past it. He seemed old, and even a little sweet.' Susan looked sad.

'Those men never change. Although they might appear to be past it, we have to remember they didn't get where they are by sitting back and letting others take charge. They are devious and manipulative, as well as being ruthless, especially when it comes to getting what they want. Money and power. Aurelio suited his purpose, because he appeared to be pleasant and clever, masking his true character. The final straw for Don Saconne was when Peppino created this sort of fearful persona, Il Gattopardo, the Leopard. It was meant to instill fear into the gangs of youths who worked around the inner suburbs of Palermo. A mysterious figure who would kill or maim if you didn't follow his rules. Don Saconne was so angry that he had used the family crest in such a violent way.'

'But the family is violent,' Susan answered. 'Why be upset by something that is true?' The commissario laughed.... 'That crest was a symbol of power, over one hundred years ago. It showed their ancestors in a poor light. All an illusion of course. They were peasants who through some lucky alliances were able to lift themselves out of poverty and parade themselves as a type of aristocracy. But you can never change a leopard's spots,' he said jokingly. 'So there you have it.... As much as we've been able to piece together, so far.'

He sat back in his chair looking at them both. 'Oh, by the way Susan, the husband of your friend Lucie, played a small part in this too. He had been exiled in Malta, as you know. He was part of a rival family that had fallen out with the Saconnes. He had made some questionable choices and was run out of town. Giovanni provided some valuable information to the police about Peppino's plans. I don't know how or where he picked it up, but we spoke to a few people, and in exchange for his information, Don Saconne and the other family reached an uneasy agreement and he was allowed to come back. Let's hope the truce lasts…we'll see…..I'm not holding my breath though.'

'Oh! Poor Lucie, I hope he manages to stay out of trouble, she's been through enough!'

'Anything else that you'd like to know? I also want to thank you both, you've been remarkably brave, and Susan your holiday hasn't really gone to plan has it?'

Susan laughed, 'well I have certainly learnt a few things. One of which is, that I can be strong and resilient when I need to be.'

'What will happen to Aurelio? Will he go to prison?'

'I don't know Angela, if he has a good lawyer he will probably get off.'

'Don Saconne will continue, as usual. Once again there is not enough actual proof to prosecute, which is not surprising. Gianni and Peppino are dead. Many of the answers we needed have gone with them. The Libyan business man has disappeared, so all we have left are the small fry, the leftovers who seem to take the fall for everyone else. They'll go to jail for a few months, maybe, and when they come out things will go back to how they were before. Don Saconne will find a new enforcer and Aurelio will represent the new generation of crime bosses, sophisticated and educated.

Refugees will keep risking their lives to make the perilous journey across the sea…. The hope of a safe and better life driving them on……..

Chapter 26

Susan spent two months working with Sister Annuncia at the refugee centre in Syracuse. It was an experience that went a long way in helping heal her trauma after finding the murdered refugees off Isola Bella. After leaving the centre, she made her way home to her children in Australia. She plans to go back to Syracuse next year to help again, this time with her daughters. She keeps in touch with Commissario Lombardo through regular emails and before she left to go back to Australia they had dinner together in Palermo.

Commissario Luca Lombardo continues to fight crime and spends his spare time working with the disadvantaged. He keeps in regular touch with Susan.

Angela is continuing with her Italian literature studies and also hosts a weekly arts program on local television. She rarely sees Aurelio and is currently going out with an architect, also from Palermo.

Aurelio spends his time travelling around Europe and beyond, working on business deals and living the life of a privileged jetsetter. He is not married.

Don Saccone continues to live in his beautiful villa in Terrasini, looked after by his loyal staff and is still calling the shots.

Lucie and her husband still live in Bagheria. He has managed to keep on a straight path and has set up a small trattoria where Lucie cooks her popular dishes. Last month she and Giovanni travelled to Naples for the first time, to see their new grandchild.